AUDACITY JONES

JONES

TO THE RESCUE

Also by Kirby Larson

NOVELS

Dash

Duke

Dear America: *The Fences Between Us*

The Friendship Doll

Hattie Big Sky

Hattie Ever After

PICTURE BOOKS

WITH MARY NETHERY

Nubs: The True Story of a Mutt, a Marine & a Miracle

Two Bobbies: A True Story of Hurricane Katrina, Friendship, and Survival

Kirby Larson

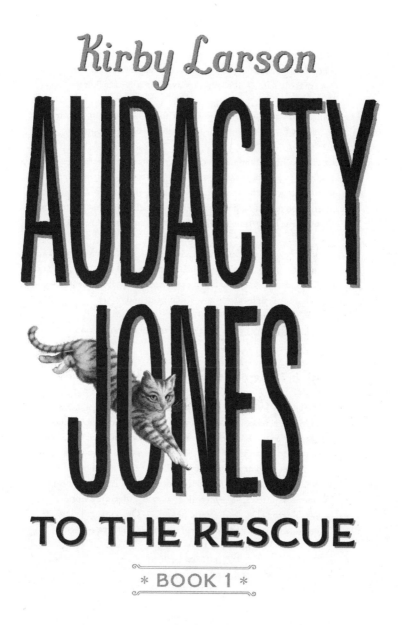

AUDACITY JONES

TO THE RESCUE

✱ BOOK 1 ✱

Scholastic Press / New York

Library of Congress Cataloging-in-Publication Data

Larson, Kirby, author.
Audacity Jones to the Rescue / Kirby Larson.—First edition.
pages cm
Summary: Audacity Jones is an eleven-year-old orphan living a monotonous life at Miss Maisie's School for Wayward Girls, and wondering why nothing exciting ever happens—but when the mysterious Commodore Crutchfield whisks her away to Washington D.C., she finds herself involved in a sinister and dangerous plot against the president of the United States.
ISBN 978-0-545-84056-9 (jacketed hardcover) 1. Orphans—Juvenile fiction. 2. Conspiracies—Juvenile fiction. 3. Adventure stories. 4. Washington (D.C.)—Juvenile fiction. [1. Orphans—Fiction. 2. Conspiracies—Fiction. 3. Adventure and adventurers—Fiction. 4. Washington (D.C.)—Fiction.] I. Title.
PZ7.L32394Au 2016
[Fic]—dc23
2015015919

10 9 8 7 6 5 4 3 2 1   16 17 18 19 20

Printed in the U.S.A.   23
First edition, February 2016

Book design by Carol Ly

*For Esme: With much love
and no squalor*

WARNING

If you are a reader whose knees wobble at the mere mention of adventure, danger, and derring-do, close these covers immediately and select a tome more to your liking.

Perhaps something about pudding.

CHAPTER ONE

The Punishment Room

Audacity Jones had once again devoured every sprig of burned broccoli, even though clean plates simply were not tolerated at Miss Maisie's School for Wayward Girls.

Miss Maisie's barley-water breath traveled the length of the scarred mahogany table, arriving well before her reprimand.

"Audacity!" The headmistress's shrill voice put a stopper on the lunchtime whispers and giggles of the Wayward Girls. "What can you be thinking?"

"I'm terribly sorry, Miss Maisie." Audacity hung her head. "I suppose this means the Punishment Room," she added, her brown eyes brimming with melancholy.

Miss Maisie's attention was diverted by a particularly succulent morsel of tinned salmon. "What? Oh yes. I suppose it does."

"But it's Christmas Eve!" chorused the triplets, Lilac, Lavender, and Violet, who could not contain their tears.

"Serves you right," Divinity snipped, a peevish gleam of joy in her piggish eyes.

"It can't be helped." Audacity—Audie to her friends—cast a resigned but courageous smile at the triplets. "I broke the rule. And so I must bear the punishment."

"Buck up, Audie girl," whispered Bimmy.

Our heroine acknowledged Bimmy's words with a brave nod. The tap-tap-tap of her black boots, two sizes too small, echoed pitifully through the dining room of Miss Maisie's family's formerly grand home, now as shabby as Audie's footwear.

* * *

For decades, the Withertons had stood tall in the town of Swayzee, Indiana, but that was before Miss Maisie's mother and father perished at sea. When the news of her parents' fate reached her, Miss Maisie wallowed in self-pity for weeks. *Months.* "Whatever shall I do?" she fretted.

Then one dark and stormy night, an equally self-absorbed young couple selling baked goods had some trouble with a balky horse near the Manor. Miss Maisie could not turn them away, not when they carried chocolate pound cakes along with a babe in arms. She allowed them to seek refuge in one of the mansion's many spare bedrooms.

Upon rising at her usual hour of noon, however, Miss Maisie was stunned to find Cook dandling the youngster on her knee and no sign of the couple except for a note enclosing a thick stack of large bills. The note merely said, *Her name is Divinity. She is too wayward for us.*

Thus the first pupil—and Miss Maisie's favorite—was enrolled in the School for Wayward Girls, where most of the girls were neither wayward nor schooled except through the latest fad in education: Professor Teachtest's Apple Core Method. Even Divinity had to admit that without Audie's stories to make the dreary lessons and relentless testing palatable, Professor Teachtest's Method would have turned each Wayward mind to mush. The Professor could not be reached to defend himself: He was in the process of purchasing his third villa in Tuscany.

Now, as Audie passed through the cracked archway into the great hall, she hesitated. "I suppose I shan't come out until breakfast."

Miss Maisie paused, forkful of beef Stroganoff to her lips. "What? Oh, well, yes. I imagine so."

Bimmy gasped, "But she'll miss her Christmas Eve treat." Every year, without fail, the Ladies' Aid Society of the Swayzee Methodist Church sent each of the Girls an orange to celebrate the Lord's birth. The basket laden with the tropically scented fruit had arrived that very morning.

Miss Maisie waved her hand. "She can have it for breakfast tomorrow." She pushed the forkful into her mouth and, sputtering gravy and beef bits all over the damask tablecloth, commanded, "Off you go."

"Yes, Miss Maisie," was our heroine's stoic reply. She skirted the drooping Christmas tree, decorated with languid paper chains, before turning left at the third cabbage rose on the well-worn carpet. Audie followed footprints she'd made the day before and the day before that and countless days before that.

After twenty long steps, Audie found herself face-to-face with the heavy mahogany portal to the Punishment Room. She was the only one of the Girls ever sent to this place; generally, Miss Maisie dealt with infractions in other ways. But Audie had been a Problem from her first moment at the School. And special circumstances called for special treatment.

Audie paused as she confronted the solid wooden door. Great carved snakes slithered from the top rail to the bottom. Each panel featured a different mythical monster; having experienced a small growth spurt, Audie was now eye-to-eye with a cyclops. Slowly, slowly, she turned the blackened brass knob and with great effort pulled the massive door open. Meanwhile, back in the dining room, Miss Maisie's attention had been fully diverted by the toffee custard that Cook had prepared for dessert.

Taking in a great breath, the girl stepped through the foreboding doorway. Quick as a flicker, Audie locked herself in, nice and tight.

When Mr. Witherton, Miss Maisie's father, had been alive, this room had not been deemed the Punishment Room, but the library. As a young lass, Miss Maisie considered every moment spent in the library to be pure agony. She had no use for the dry and dusty books that lined the walls, from the tip-top of the coved ceiling to the worn oak floorboards. "Words, words, words," she would grumble when her father invited her in.

"Perhaps *Jane Eyre*, or *Persuasion*," Mr. Witherton would suggest. "Or, my favorite, *A Tale of Two Cities*?"

"No, no, and no," Miss Maisie would answer, time and again. "Books are utter wastes of paper that could be put to better uses, like wrappings for presents for me."

Mr. Witherton did love his daughter, but as he and his wife had gurgled down to Davy Jones's locker that fateful day, he had mused, *Well, I shall never have the disappointment of Maisie turning down a book again, shall I?* That thought provided soggy comfort until an unfortunate encounter with not one ravenous bull shark but two.

On this winter night, as was her habit from the time Mr. Witherton was still in residence, Cook had laid a fire in the grand Dutch-tiled fireplace, with one match set by. Because she had read through Mr. Witherton's copious collection of books on survival in the wilds, one match was all Audie needed to nourish a warm blaze, which soon chased the chill from the bright and windowed room. As also was her habit, Cook had set a plate of Gouda, ginger-snaps, and grapes on the table next to the reading chair, for Mr. Witherton had so appreciated a tasty treat while he read.

Audie nibbled on a gingersnap while pondering which section of the vast and varied library to tackle next. Her eye was drawn to Horton Halfpott's forty-volume memoir, a series our dear girl found compelling, even after numerous readings.

Or should she read about South American botany, complete with references to poisonous plants? Some were undetectable even in toffee custard. Not that *she* would ever harm a soul. Revenge was beneath Audie's dignity, though Divinity had provoked her to drastic action at times. But we shall refrain from mentioning the incidents with the live toad and the dead garter snake.

As Audie contemplated which of the hundreds of books to select, Miniver wriggled in through one small leaded-glass window, left enough ajar for the sleek cat to come and go as she pleased. The chocolate-striped feline immediately set to licking clumps of snow from her paws. Cat and girl had been fast friends since Audie's arrival at Miss Maisie's five years prior, when Audie was a slip of a six-year-old carrying a stuffed giraffe named Percy, and Miniver a runt chased away from her mother's teats by five greedy and guzzling brothers.

Audie had been sent to the Punishment Room her first day at Miss Maisie's, not wayward, but orphaned—guardianed by an uncle who could not seem to tell the difference. He had presented Miss Maisie with a tidy sum before striding off without one backward glance at the waif who'd been in his care less than a fortnight.

Even at the tender age of six, Audie had been resourceful. In the pockets of her little pink pinafore she had stashed a nubbin of cheese and two biscuits against possible hunger. And what foresight! Shortly after Miss Maisie had dispatched Audie to the Punishment Room—her offense had been to inquire as to the location of the School's classrooms—Miniver squeezed in through the library window for the first time and was delighted to share that bit of cheese.

In the toes of Audie's kid-leather boots, once lovingly polished by her parents—her father always buffed the left, her mother, the right—rested a pair of gold coins. Not that Audie gave a fig for money, but there are many that do place great importance on silver and gold, and, as has already been mentioned, Audie was nothing if not one to plan ahead.

Her toilette now completed, Miniver padded on four snowy-white paws to greet her long-time friend with a loving head tap.

"You smell of catnip, Min," the ever-observant girl observed. "Been in Mr. Schumacher's greenhouse again, have you?" Audie tsk-tsked but Min took no offense, weaving in and out of Audie's legs as the girl slowly circled the library floor. Sharing the ginger-snap with her feline friend, Audie mused aloud about what to read next.

"I will admit to being weak in geography, Min. I know the forty-six states and the seven continents, and the seven seas, but, bees and bonnets, I can never remember the difference between Liechtenstein and Luxembourg." She took another nibble of gin-gersnap, with Min thoughtfully dispatching the crumbs. "And my mathematics are appalling. Here I am eleven and I can barely do calculus. I should be more diligent in that regard. But I have a longing, Min. A longing for something entirely different." Audie ran her fingers across the section of bookshelves that held Mr. Witherton's prodigious collection of adventure stories.

Her hand reached for a particularly exciting tale, then dropped, heart shriveling with misery. How could our intrepid girl bear to read yet one more story about those who were *not* confined to places such as Miss Maisie's, who had futures holding possibilities greater than growing as unsweet as Divinity? Where was the adventure, the challenge, the fun, for one such as Audie?

As Min was wont to do, she leapt up onto the library table, tail twitching, ready to weigh in with her own literary advice. After a nibble at the wedge of Gouda, she shifted herself around, away from Audie, to face out the window.

"Don't scold," Audie begged. "That's not in the holiday spirit."

But the cat did not budge; she had firmly turned her back on the girl.

"Oh, all right." Audie stepped toward the mathematics wall. "I shall push on with that old calculus."

Min rumbled a low-throated warning, her gaze fixed on something through the panes of leaded glass.

"Are you saying my plan doesn't meet with your approval?"

Min hissed, tail flicking sharply.

Audie stepped to the window and drew aside the dust-coated brocade draperies.

"What's the matter, Min? Now, remember, you promised to leave those thrushes alone." The girl peered out to discover what had set her friend aflutter. A touring car, painted the most charming shade of robin's egg blue, was gliding down the long drive to the house. Few vehicles ever ventured their way. And hardly any came that were of the motorized variety.

"A visitor?" Audie exclaimed. "Or perhaps another Wayward Girl?" It had been nearly two years since the last Wayward, Katy Van Aken, had joined the household. It was tight quarters for the seventeen of them but they would make room for one more. Always room for one more.

Min jumped to the nearest shelf, dislodging an entire row of books. Audie scooped them up, intent on returning them to their rightful places. She could easily resist the temptation of paging through *Mrs. Paul's Manners for the Modern Young Lady*, but it was not as easy to avoid the siren's call of the other titles: *Nethery's New World Atlas*, *The Peoples' Proverbs* by Professor Helen Moon Ketteman, *Fair Criminals, Foul Minds* by Detective P. Gardella, and *Conversational French* by D. Curtis Regan and V. Sathre.

Her reshelving task had scarcely begun when a bell sounded. It was not the doorbell, which had mysteriously ceased working the very day Mr. and Mrs. Witherton disappeared at sea, but the

Gathering Bell, which sounded when Miss Maisie gave a sharp pull on the purple velvet rope in the parlor. At that chime, the girls were trained to stop whatever they were doing and assemble in the parlor, no matter where they were in the house or yard.

Min bounded out the window.

"See you tomorrow!" Audie called. Like her fellow Waywards, she, too, ran to the parlor, unaware that she still cradled the above-mentioned titles in her arms. She was equally unaware of one other important fact: that she would not see her feline friend on the morrow.

All because of the Commodore.

CHAPTER TWO

A Mysterious Mission

Audie stashed her armful of books behind the umbrella stand in the hall and dashed to the parlor. Bimmy snatched her up in a hug as the triplets teared up all over again to see their companion returned, unscathed, from her trials and tribulations.

"Quiet, girls!" Miss Maisie cast a befuddled glance in Audie's direction. "What are you doing here?"

"Answering the Gathering Bell, Miss Maisie," Audie answered sweetly.

"You should have remained in the Punishment Room!" Miss Maisie's words unleashed the triplets' barely contained emotions. The parlor was soon noisier than the Swayzee train station.

Miss Maisie flailed her arms, fat flapping at the undersides like wrinkled pillowcases on a clothesline. "Stop that caterwauling!" Her command only served to increase the flow of tears as Violet and Lavender began boo-hooing along with their youngest-by-minutes sister. Bimmy's lower lip trembled.

Desperate for order, Miss Maisie turned to the weeping girls. "Are you all hankering a visit to the Punishment Room?"

That threat propelled the sobs to a crescendo but, with practiced skill, Audie stemmed the triplets' tide of tears, and cosseted Bimmy as well. Soon, all was as calm as a Presbyterian potluck.

Miss Maisie cleared her throat. "Girls, we have a guest. A distinguished and important guest." She lowered her voice. "So behave!" Then she turned and, with a flourish, gestured for someone to enter. "Do come in, Commodore Crutchfield!"

Accompanied by a jingle of medals, an older man, jauntily swinging a cane, sailed into the room. A dress-white admiral's hat decorated with an exquisite white rosette sat atop a head of wavy white hair long enough to brush his upturned white collar.

"Good afternoon, Commodore." Divinity led the Wayward chorus.

With a grand swoop, he bowed low in acknowledgment. "Good afternoon to you, lassies."

"We are so honored by your visit." Miss Maisie attempted a curtsy. It was not a pretty sight. "We did not expect you for some weeks yet."

Over the years, Miss Maisie had been unable to disabuse the Commodore of the idea that her school was for orphans, rather than waywards. The kindly gent insisted on presenting a check—"for the good of the lasses"—every January 19 in honor of Robert E. Lee's birthday. The Commodore was also a product of Westmoreland County, Virginia, though he had been born some forty years after the General.

"About that." The Commodore patted his vest pocket.

Miss Maisie's smile was not unlike that of a snake in contemplation of a plump and captive rodent. She stretched out her hand for the annual donation. "You are far too generous," she murmured, licking her lips. This infusion of cash would mean a five-pound box of sweets, rather than the two pounder she'd put on order with the grocer, Mr. Sharp.

"About that," he began again.

"I do hope things are going well with your business," Miss Maisie said. "Girls, remember, Commodore Crutchfield owns one of the largest factories in town—"

"In the state," he corrected.

"In Indiana," Miss Maisie continued.

It seemed odd to think that a business making silk rosettes to decorate horse bridles and footmen's livery could be so profitable. But profitable it must be, Audie decided, to judge by that fancy new town car in the drive.

"The Commodore's work is sought out by the finest gentlemen in the country." Miss Maisie tittered. "His rosettes are in great demand at the President's stable!"

"Well, at Teddy's." The Commodore ducked his head.

Miss Maisie clasped her hands under her triple chin and nearly swooned with admiration. "Such modesty!"

"Regrettably, our current President is a fiend for the automobile, rather than the equine." Their visitor patted his vest pocket again.

"Oh, that is regrettable." Miss Maisie reached her hand out again to hurry the Commodore along. Maybe five pounds of chocolates and some candied violets. That would be lovely.

Abruptly, the Commodore moved his hand from his vest to his pockets. He pulled out handfuls of small pink rosettes. "In the trade, we call them cockades, not rosettes. But by either name, here are some as gifts for your girls!" He handed them around, smiling broadly.

The girls smiled back, uncertain of what to do with the frilled circles. Divinity found a hairpin and affixed hers to her braid. Audie tucked her rosette-cockade into her pinafore pocket.

Miss Maisie's smile wobbled in her pasty face. She wondered if the Commodore had already been at the Yule eggnog. He had clearly forgotten why he'd come. She would have to help him along. "Was there something else?" she hinted broadly.

"Something else?" The Commodore's brow furrowed. "Well, yes there is. And I will get right to it." He turned his toothy white smile on Miss Maisie. "Such a pretty lot and so lovingly cared for. That is clear to see."

Miss Maisie's cheeks bloomed candy-apple pink.

Apparently, the Commodore's eyes were not as sharp as the crease in his white trousers because, had they been, he would certainly have seen that, except for Divinity, most of the Wayward Girls were dressed in ragged pinafores worn over woefully short dresses. Some, like Audie, also pinched their feet into boots several sizes too small.

Lest you think too ill of Miss Maisie, you should know that she did allot her wards a small allowance for clothing each month. But most of the Girls followed Audie's example, putting that allowance into a communal pot—in this case, a rare and expensive Ming vase. Miss Maisie's self-absorption prevented her from noticing that the

Manor was crumbling down around her. It fell to the Girls to act as caretakers of the Witherton family home. Instead of ordering new frocks and boots from the Sears, Roebuck and Co. catalog, the Girls ordered a new roof for the Manor when the old one sprang a leak. (Audie found a book on roofing in the Punishment Room and shepherded the older Waywards through the delicate repairs.) They sent for tulip bulbs in the fall and vegetable seeds in the spring to plant in the Manor gardens. And twice they'd ordered chicks that had come all the way from Rhode Island. Reds they were, and good layers.

"I do adore these girls so. As if they were my own." Miss Maisie fluttered her hands every which way. "Why, just this morning, I was telling little Violet here—"

"I'm Lilac."

"How I hoped she would never leave us."

The Commodore bowed again. "I can see that the bond between you and your charges is as robust as the ropes that lash the mainsail together."

"The mainsail?" The question popped out of Audie's mouth before she could stop it.

The Commodore chuckled. "Nautical term, my dear. Nautical term. Comes from a career in Uncle Sam's navy."

"Children do not speak until spoken to," Miss Maisie said. "Audie. Dear."

Again the Commodore chuckled. "No harm. No harm." He stroked the white caterpillar moustache atop his lip. "As I was saying, it is clear that you are the light of these orphans' lives and that they are the light of yours."

Again Miss Maisie's hands flitted about. "Well, they are the dearest little—"

"So what I have come to ask will require you to be brave, my dear. To be bold." He cleared his throat and lowered his voice. "God and country; for the greater good and all that."

"I'm not sure I understand." On the best day, Miss Maisie's mind could readily be compared to a steel trap. One that was rusted shut.

The Commodore motioned her close, but spoke with volume enough for all the girls to hear. "I need help with an important job. Supremely hush-hush." He placed a well-manicured finger to his lips. "But deucedly important."

"Well, I couldn't leave my charges, not at the holidays," Miss Maisie started. "And I haven't yet finished dessert. Toffee custard."

"Oh, my dear." The Commodore descended upon Miss Maisie's puffy hand and bestowed it with a kiss.

Miss Maisie launched into a remarkably apt imitation of a carp. Her plump lips swam up and down but not a burble emerged from between them.

"I would never presume to ask *you* to leave this place and the good work you are doing here." The Commodore swept his cape over his shoulder with drama and finesse. "I am here to solicit a volunteer. For a mission."

"Mission?" The word worked its way out of Miss Maisie's gyrating mouth.

"Mission?" Seventeen girlish voices echoed their headmistress.

"I may not say more." The Commodore held up his hand. "It is a matter of utmost secrecy. And"—he leaned in toward Miss Maisie's ear—"discretion."

"Sounds dangerous." Divinity squinted at the Commodore.

For once, Audie agreed with her nemesis.

He gave a quick nod. "There is always danger for those who are afraid of it."

"George Bernard Shaw," said Audie with a nod of her own.

The Commodore took her in with a sharp glance. "Why, yes. Those *are* his words."

"I don't like danger," said Bimmy. "Too dangerous."

"I agree," said Lilac. Her two sisters began to sniffle. The other girls began to ape Miss Maisie's carp impression. Sixteen mouths opened and closed, wordlessly.

But the seventeenth mouth formed a tight, straight line.

"What about this orphan here?" The Commodore indicated the newest of the Wayward Girls. Katy shrank back, hiding behind Audie. The Commodore continued in a coaxing voice, "You can ride in my fine new automobile!"

"I get carsick," Katy said. "At least, I'm pretty sure I do."

"Well, what about that orphan?" He aimed a polished pinky at Emma.

"I don't speak English," Emma said.

"What about—" the Commodore began again.

"Excuse me, Commodore." Miss Maisie stepped forward, her right hand fidgeting with the butterfly brooch on her ample bosom. "Did you say 'orphan'?"

"This is an orphanage, is it not?"

Miss Maisie chuckled good-naturedly. "Oh, I'm afraid you are confused." How many times did she have to remind the old crackpot?

She smiled forgiveness. "A frequent misperception. This is a school for the wayward, not the orphaned."

"There are *no* orphans here?" His white moustache fairly drooped.

"No. Dear me." Miss Maisie pressed her hands to her doughy cheeks. "I am so sorry, after all, that we cannot render assistance with your admirable efforts."

Divinity tugged on the Commodore's white jacket. "She is." Her stubby index finger pointed straight at Audie. "An orphan." Divinity's blue eyes crackled with spite.

Long accustomed to Divinity's torments, Audie did not flinch from being so identified.

"A minor detail." Miss Maisie dismissed Divinity's revelation. "She's more wayward than all the rest put together. Far too much trouble . . ." Her voice trailed off. The headmistress sorely lacked the mental acuity necessary to forestall the outcome of Divinity's action.

Audie stared first at Divinity and then at the Commodore. He could not hold her gaze long and broke away.

"Are you an orphan?" He was particularly anxious about the reply because this lass looked as if she were up to the task.

Audie nodded. Our heroine was ever truthful, no matter the consequence. Whether or not this is a trait to admire I shall leave to your judgment, dear reader.

"Will you do it, then?" the Commodore asked.

She considered. It was true that she had been longing for an adventure. But was that sufficient reason to go off with a naval man, no matter how wealthy, who seemed to have no idea that mainsails were never lashed together with ropes? Or that the rank of Commodore had last been used by the United States Navy eleven years prior, in 1899? The answer to both of these questions is, of course, no.

And that would have been Audie's answer, too, save for the buzzing in her left ear. That buzzing was a phenomenon she had learned *not* to ignore. If only her parents had listened to her, and begged off on that safari in the Dutch East Indies when she was five—her ear had nearly buzzed right off her head that day—she might not be in this current predicament.

More prudent minds might label the Commodore's request nothing more than a wild-goose chase. But what good are wild geese, if not pursued upon occasion? Audie reflected on a Chinese proverb she'd skimmed in *The People's Proverbs*: "Pearls don't lie on the seashore. If you desire one, you must dive for it." In her short life, she had noted that, oftimes, a person is put in difficult positions for good reasons. Reasons that are beyond comprehension. And more than having an adventure, Audie dreamed of doing some good in the world. It appeared that in order to gather that particular pearl, she would have to dive. "Bees and bonnets," she said. "I'll go."

"Well then. We're off." The Commodore replaced his hat atop his head. "Come along . . . lassie."

"You're leaving now?" Miss Maisie looked befuddled. "Tomorrow is Christmas Day."

"The young lady and I have a date with destiny," he said. "No time to lose."

The triplets' sniffles exploded into wails. Bimmy threw her arms around Audie's waist. "Don't go, Audie. Don't!"

Audie patted her comrade's back. "What have I always told you?" she asked.

Bimmy released her grip, drawing in a shaky breath. "That everything will turn out splendid in the end," she said. "And if it's not splendid, it's not the end."

Audie chucked Bimmy under the chin. "That's the ticket. No need to worry about me," she asserted, though, truth be told, her voice conveyed more confidence than she felt.

"Oh, I won't," said Miss Maisie, wondering if it would be rude to slip out to the kitchen for an éclair. All of this excitement had left her feeling peckish.

"We will!" chorused the triplets, on the verge once again of imitating Niagara Falls. Audie staunched their waterworks with comforting hugs and then turned to face the Commodore. "It won't take me but a jiff to pack."

Farewells were made as Audie gathered her belongings, including the books she'd stashed behind the umbrella stand. Her pinafore was soggy with the triplets' tears by the time the last of her meager possessions was packed in a worn carpetbag loaned her by none other than Divinity.

"Good riddance," were Divinity's tender words of parting.

There were no words spoken aloud between Audie and Bimmy, merely a shared hug and a whisper from Audie into her bosom chum's ear.

With a wave to Miss Maisie, in whose frilled bodice was safely tucked a promissory note for an exorbitant sum given her by the Commodore for the "loan of a brave little orphan lass," Audie climbed into the touring car.

Sadly, there was not even time for a quick *adieu* to Miniver, but Audie had no worries about the plucky cat, as resourceful and resilient as Audie herself.

CHAPTER THREE

A Friend in Need

A long-limbed feline, her coat a lush robe of chocolate stripes, blinked two gold eyes at the fancy automobile. A large man, all in white, like an angel or a phantom, slid his portly self into the passenger's side of the front seat. Another man, with hair as black as a raven's wing and the scent of the desert about him, tested the rear passenger door handles. They were locked.

The cat undulated her long dark tail ever so slowly. In that instant, the man from the desert worried that he had forgotten to lock the latches on the wicker trunk fastened at the rear of the vehicle. He stepped around to check. Locked. But perhaps he should make certain they were latched properly. He undid the locks, and the cat flicked her tail again. Was it by mere coincidence that a puff of wind caught the chauffeur's cap at that exact instant, sending said cap tumbling down the drive? We leave it to you to judge. At any rate, the man gave chase rather a goodly distance—it was a shockingly vigorous gust. His breathing was ragged by the time he returned, cap firmly settled on his shiny black hair. He then completed the task of locking the wicker trunk, giving each latch a tug to check its security before proceeding to the driver's door.

"Odd about that wind," the man in white observed. "Came out of nowhere."

The dark-haired man nodded in agreement. "This hat cost me three dollars. I wasn't about to lose it." After a long spate of bad luck, the man had only recently found this employment opportunity as a chauffeur. He was eager for his first paycheck, which would help him recoup the cost of said cap and the rest of his snappy driver's uniform.

"Shall we be off, then, the three of us?" the man in white suggested.

"Yes, sir." The driver gave the engine a good many cranks, then took his seat behind the wheel. He drove cautiously down the rutted lane, under the gray flannel afternoon sky, completely unaware that the vehicle now carried not three but four passengers, one of whom was curled up in a wicker trunk next to a well-worn carpetbag, where she was carefully bathing each of her four white paws.

CHAPTER FOUR

1600 Pennsylvania Avenue

"Oh, Father, do we have to?" Charlie kicked at the legs of the chair upon which he was perched. Never mind that Abraham Lincoln might have occupied that very chair. The young lad was too peeved to think about the historic import of White House furnishings. He kicked harder. "We're barely related."

President Taft turned his blue eyes on his youngest child. "Charlie, you may recall the pleasant hours you passed in this place when Quentin Roosevelt was in your shoes. I would hope you would be as generous a host."

Mrs. Taft set her fork down. "The roast is delicious tonight, isn't it, Will?" Her speech was so clear you would never have guessed she'd suffered a stroke mere months before. "Mrs. Jaffray has outdone herself."

Her husband nodded.

Mrs. Taft sighed, her face awash in dreaminess. "How well I recall *my* first White House visit. At seventeen." Her fingers grazed the violets pinned to her bodice, releasing their delicate fragrance.

"One step inside and I was smitten." She smiled sweetly. "I made a wish then and there that I might live in the White House someday. Thank you, my dear, for making that wish come true."

The President returned her smile and then nudged aside a piece of gristle with his knife. He pointed said knife at his son. "She'll only be here for a few days." He lifted a large bite of beef, dripping with gravy, to his mouth. "And she *is* your cousin." He chewed thoughtfully. "Of sorts. And said to be quite spirited and charming."

"But she's a *girl*, Father." Charlie threw his napkin onto the table, ignoring his mother's uplifted eyebrows. "A boring old girl."

President Taft chuckled. "I remember thinking along those same lines about the female of the species. Until that delightful sledding outing with your mother." He gazed adoringly at his wife, unaware of the drop of gravy glistening on his chin.

"Father!" Charlie's head thumped to the table. "Now you've made me ill."

Mrs. Taft pantomimed wiping her chin. Her husband did not get the message. She cleared her throat, pointing discreetly.

"Cousins can turn out to be the best of friends," the President boomed, brushing away the offending drop. "Even girls. Especially girls."

Charlie's head lifted from the tabletop one inch. "Please don't make me." In his mind's eye, he foresaw endless games of hopscotch and charades and other deadly dull pastimes.

His father calmly and methodically cleaned up the remaining bits of beef and potato on the plate. "Of course, I won't make you."

Charlie sat upright. He felt the wings of freedom sprouting at his shoulders. "Really, Father?"

The elder Taft leaned back, patting his stout midsection before dabbing his mouth with a monogrammed linen napkin. He rang the bell for after-dinner coffee. (Never port; this president had foresworn alcohol.) *"I* won't make you," Charlie's father repeated, liberally spooning sugar into his coffee cup. He toasted his wife. "Your mother will."

If his mother was behind cousin Dorothy's visit, there was no hope. No way out. Charlie was doomed. Doomed.

His heart turned to lead with the weight of this unbearable sentence. "May I be excused?"

"You may," his parents chorused.

At that, Charles Phelps Taft removed himself from the dining room with as much dignity as any condemned man could muster.

Because that is what he was.

Condemned to entertaining his twelve-year-old distant cousin, Dorothy, for two entire days of his Christmas vacation.

CHAPTER FIVE

Heading Toward the Rising Sun

The touring car bumped down West Lyons Street, and past the Swayzee Depot, where a Toledo, St. Louis, and Western Railway train was groaning into the station. As the auto rumbled down Washington, toward the outskirts of town, Audie kept herself busy trying to identify as many of the passing trees as possible: ash, dogwood, birch. There, in front of the town grammar school, a white pine was stooped over like an old woman, limbs sagging with the weight of the previous night's freezing rain. Several blocks farther along, a stray dog limped to shelter under the livery stable overhang. It watched the touring car pass, scratching its ear all the while. Audie wiggled her fingers in greeting.

The voyagers continued under an icy sky and Audie was grateful for the thick wool blanket draped over her legs. Jack Frost nipped cruelly at her cheeks and nose. What she wouldn't give for a matching muff and hat like that girl across the way, walking with her family up the front steps of the Catholic church.

Tucking deeper under the lap blanket, Audie pushed aside thoughts of personal discomfort. Having availed herself of Mr. Witherton's many atlases over the years, she surmised that the touring car was now jostling south toward Dayton, Ohio.

She tested that observation on the Commodore. "Are we heading to Dayton?" she inquired.

"Oh, dear, Annie." The Commodore rotated with great effort to look at her as he spoke. "Do not trouble your pretty little head about such things. We are in good hands with Cypher here at the wheel. And all is going to plan." At that, the Commodore gave a little chuckle. "Yes. Everything's aces and eights," he proclaimed giddily.

Audie wondered if the Commodore was aware that "aces and eights" was not something to evoke cheer. It was the Dead Man's Hand, the very cards Mr. Wild Bill Hickok held when he was murdered in a most cowardly fashion. She'd read about it in one of Mr. Witherton's books. "Aces and eights were an unlucky combination for Wild Bill Hickok," she began, but her efforts at conversation were stymied by a loud snore. The Commodore had dozed off.

And now he had been imitating a bull moose the last many miles. The driver, Cypher, had thus far deflected any of Audie's efforts at chitchat, so it seemed unlikely *he* would answer her questions about their ultimate destination. The thought came into her mind that, once they reached Indianapolis, they'd head east on the Old

National Road. This notion set her left ear abuzzing like a clutch of gossiping busybodies. So east they must be going.

Of course, a hunch was not completely to be trusted. And yet— there had been too many times that little ear buzz had proven prophetic. There was the tragic example of her own parents' demise. And then again, when she had been at Miss Maisie's for less than a year, she'd awakened in the wee hours of April 18, screaming, "The earth is shaking! The earth is shaking!" Swayzee had been unscathed but that same day the entire city of San Francisco collapsed under a great earthquake and fire. And Audie was the talk of the School when she anticipated the Great Chocolate Shortage of 1908, saving each of the Wayward Girls from Miss Maisie's ill humors by stashing away bits and nibs of cocoa against such a catastrophe. As has already been mentioned, Audie was a girl with foresight.

Now, as she shifted on the tufted seat, she grew convinced of two things. One, that this touring car *would* head east, perhaps as far east as this great country's capital. And, two, that it had been a huge mistake to allow her bag to be packed away at the rear of the touring car, in the trunk.

What she wouldn't give for a book in her hands right now, though she would be required to strain to read in the fading light. The monotony of an etiquette book like *Mrs. Paul's Manners for the Modern Young Lady* would be livelier than staring out at the ice-sculptured landscape. Audie sighed, rearranging the wool blanket over her legs. She was desperate enough to settle for a calculus primer.

A parade of farms and pastures and villages galloped past. She couldn't be sure—she had yet to begin a study of physics—but she suspected they were traveling in excess of fifteen miles per hour, when the occasional cow did not hinder their progress. Fifteen miles an hour! In eight hours of travel, they could make it all the way to Ohio.

If it were summer, Audie might have asked the chauffeur to stop in Cicero, so she could cool her toes in the lake there. But this was winter. No swimming. Perhaps the lake was frozen solid enough for skating! She remembered back to a time when Papa had held her left hand and Mama her right and they had cut delicate triple figure eights on Grier's Pond. She had only been three but she could still recall the *shhhh* of their skate blades slicing through the ice in unison; she could still feel her parents' warmth through her knitted woolen mittens.

Pressing her palms together in the backseat, Audie glanced again at the driver. There was a sternness to the back of his head—neck stiff, cap settled just so. He did not seem the type to indulge a young orphan in her desire to recapture a precious childhood memory. Not even at Christmastime. Along with his striking appearance, the driver gave off the aura of one who would not indulge a young girl's desire in any shape or form. In fact, she had the most definite sensation that his preference would have been that Audie had remained at Miss Maisie's. Some adults simply are not fond of children. It is the sad but bitter truth.

Audie returned her gaze outside the moving auto. The rhythm of the rackety engine and the scenery whizzing past had an almost hypnotic effect. It wasn't until the engine was shut off that she started, aware that she'd fallen asleep. For how long, she did not know. But it was extremely dark. And extremely cold.

"Here we are." The Commodore unfolded himself from the front seat and stepped out. He paused, stretching and moaning once he was upright on two feet again. "Our lodgings for the night."

Audie blinked the sleep from her eyes and focused on the clapboard building in front of her. A hand-painted sign proclaimed, THE LYON'S DEN HOTEL: BEST IN OHIO.

"Wait here," the driver ordered. "And when we fetch you, do not speak unless spoken to."

"Cypher, cast aside your worries." The Commodore arranged his cloak over his shoulders. "Annie will be no trouble."

"Audie." She said her name firmly. "Actually, it's Audacity."

Cypher gave the Commodore a satisfied look.

"Audie." The Commodore corrected himself with a chuckle. "Of course, my dear. Of course." He and Cypher made their way to the front door of the hotel. Cypher held it open to allow the Commodore to enter first.

Audie pulled the wool blanket around her, a worthless shield against the cold night air. They had been riding since lunchtime. Her back ached. Her legs ached. Her sit-upon especially ached. Would her traveling companions be any the wiser if she got out and stretched?

She reached for the door handle and pulled. Stuck. Or locked? With a careful glance toward the hotel, she snaked her arm over the top edge of the door frame, feeling for the outer handle. She patted around until her fingers touched metal and then she grabbed hold and tugged. The handle didn't budge. Somehow, it was locked from both the inside and out. Why were they so keen on keeping her in the car?

Audie flopped back, shivering. An icebox would be warmer than her current environment. And her stomach was indignant in its demand for nourishment. It now occurred to Audie that adventure could be highly overrated.

After what seemed like hours, Cypher returned, unlocking the door. "You'll carry your own bag," he said, with a jerk of the head toward the hotel. "I've got to manage his."

"I don't m-m-mind," Audie answered, teeth chattering. She followed Cypher to the rear of the automobile, clutching her coat around her while he undid the latches on the wicker trunk.

A gust of wind tumbled Cypher's hat from his head. "Not again!" He cursed vociferously before giving chase. Audie couldn't help but smile to see the hat zig when he zagged. Without taking her eyes from the unfolding drama, she opened the trunk and pulled out her bag. Her fingers brushed against something furry.

Hope floated her heart like a balloon. "Min?" She peered through the dark into the trunk. But all she could see was the Commodore's fur coat. Of course, any reasonable person would realize how ridiculous to have thought otherwise.

Though it seems difficult to believe, Cypher's mood was sourer still when he returned, perspiration dripping down his angular face. "Come on." He snatched up the rest of the bags and slammed the wicker trunk's lid shut. In his snit, he didn't bother to latch it back up, much to the good fortune of the unseen occupant. Audie picked up her bag and books and followed him.

The Lyon's Den was tidy and, most important to Audie at that juncture, warm. The ruddy-faced proprietress, Mrs. O'Connor, fussed over her, whipping up a mug of hot milk with honey to drink during the final preparations of a late supper.

"This is delicious." Audie patted her mouth with a napkin. "Thank you so much."

"Your niece has such pretty manners," Mrs. O'Connor told the Commodore.

Cypher coughed.

"She attends Miss Maisie's Finishing School for Fine Young Ladies," the Commodore replied. "You've heard of it, of course."

"Of course." Mrs. O'Connor nodded as if only the most hayseedy of hayseeds would not have heard of the School.

Audie stifled back any comment of her own with a yawn.

"Oh, you poor lamb." Mrs. O'Connor set down the platter of sandwiches she held. "You must be done in. Let me show you to your lodgings."

Audie followed Mrs. O'Connor's broad beam up a narrow set of stairs to a room tucked under the eaves. When the door was opened, Audie gasped.

Mrs. O'Connor clucked her tongue. "I know it's not what you're used to, darlin', but I do think you'll find it cozy."

Audie shook her head. "It's . . . perfect." After sharing a room with half a dozen other girls all these years, a *cupboard* to herself would have been sheer pleasure. But a room like this—with crisp Priscilla curtains at the window, and a sunny yellow quilt on a bed topped with two plump pillows—was close to heaven on earth.

Mrs. O'Connor laughed. "Ah, go on with you." But inwardly she made a note that should she ever have both a daughter and the funds, she would send her to Miss Maisie's Finishing School. If Audie was any example, Miss Maisie clearly turned out the kindest and most well-mannered young women east of the Mississippi. "Do you fancy a hot bath before bed?"

"Oh, yes, please!" Adventure be hanged! Audie hoped she would never, ever have to leave the Lyon's Den.

Nearly an hour later, with her hair in damp curls and her fingers raisined from a deliciously long soak, Audie emerged from the bathroom and made her way to her charming chamber.

The door to the Commodore's room was closed tight, but proved an insufficient barrier to his powerful snoring. Cypher's door was ajar; Audie shivered. Who knew how a slumber-time encounter with that man might impact her dreams? She turned away from his room toward the stairs, which cast a welcoming light from down at the end of the long, dark hall. Audie grabbed a handful of flannel nightie, lifting the hem so that she wouldn't trip. Odd that Mrs. O'Connor thought of so many comforts, but not to light a lodger's way to bed.

A murmuring caught Audie's attention and she froze. There was much she could not make out but one sentence pounced upon her ear.

"We need to get the girl out of the picture."

Cypher! He was on the telephone in the hallway. To whom was he speaking? And was she the girl to be removed from the picture? But that made no sense. The Commodore had said she was needed. For a mission of great import. Audie yawned, tired to the marrow of her bones. The last thing she needed in this state was to let her imagination run away with her.

She once again tiptoed on her way to those inviting stairs. But one of the toes on which she tiptoed—the largest on the left foot—made unfortunate contact with an oak coat tree Mrs. O'Connor had inherited from her grandmother. "Bees and bonnets!" Audie hopped up and down, eyes stinging with pain. "That hurt."

Despite the attention being demanded by her throbbing big toe, Audie sensed a change in the hallway. A wariness. Then the softest of *thwicks* as a telephone receiver was replaced in its cradle and then the sense of a desert breeze wafting past her. Audie turned in time to see the door to Cypher's room close, slowly but firmly. How had he passed her unseen? No doubt while she was hopping around, hollering like a banshee because of her toe. No matter.

"Sweet dreams to you, too, Mr. Cypher." Audie climbed the stairs, where she promptly crawled under the yellow quilt, blew out the lamp, and was soon a contented visitor to Dreamland in the cheerful room at the top of the stairs.

CHAPTER SIX

A Nose for News

*"Merry Christmas!" Mrs. O'Connor greeted Audie as she padded, sleepy-*eyed, to the dining room for breakfast. The proprietress was hanging an evergreen wreath in the window.

"Merry Christmas to you, too." Audie felt a little pang, imagining the holiday activities back at Miss Maisie's. Cook would have baked cinnamon rolls; Audie hoped Bimmy would remember to limit the triplets to two apiece. Then, after a hearty breakfast of eggs and ham, the household would gather 'round the tree to open gifts. No doubt, there would be seventeen somethings from Miss Maisie, identical and identically useless. Last year, each girl had been given a roller skate key. Never mind that no one owned any roller skates. Cook would pass around something sweet: a bag of horehound drops, peppermint sticks, or perhaps lollipops. Audie was sorry to miss that, certainly, but she was most sorry to miss the reactions to her *gift* to her Wayward companions: Using instructions discovered in one of Mr. Witherton's books, she'd made seventeen paper kites—including one for herself—ready to sail on the first dry, windy day of spring. She wondered: Would she be back from her adventure in time to join them?

Mrs. O'Connor placed a mug brimming with rich hot chocolate in front of Audie. She returned the chocolate pot to the stove, wiped her hands on her apron, and presented Audie with a small package. "Santy Claus finds you, no matter how far you are from home." She turned to the Commodore. "The little lass needs some'at to open this morning! Especially when she's parted from her mum and dad!"

The Commodore signaled Audie not to correct Mrs. O'Connor.

"Oh, I couldn't." Audie stared at the gift on her plate, tied up in a swatch of gingham.

"Of course you could." Mrs. O'Connor hovered behind her. "Go on now."

The Commodore nodded his approval.

Audie untied the fabric wrapping to reveal a book. "Oh, thank you!"

"I thought you'd enjoy it." Mrs. O'Connor smoothed her apron over and over. "You being such a reader and all."

Audie stroked the cover. *Little Women.* "I will treasure it always. Always."

"Bought it some years back, with an eye to save it for my children," Mrs. O'Connor said. "But seeings as I don't have any of my own, and here you turn up at the holidays, well, it all seems to fit together like a puzzle, don't it?" She reached her hand out as if to smooth Audie's hair, then drew it back. "Now, eat before it all gets cold." Mrs. O'Connor foisted roll upon bacon rasher upon soft-boiled egg on Audie. "Your niece needs fattening up," she informed the Commodore.

"Niece?" He glanced up from his third stack of pancakes, wearing a maple-syrup-induced glaze in his eyes.

"She's a scarecrow, she is," scolded Mrs. O'Connor. "Wants more meat on her bones."

The Commodore finished swallowing. "I've never seen her tuck in the way she has this morning. It's your cooking, Mrs. O'Connor."

A bit of pink brightened Mrs. O'Connor's plump cheeks. "Oh, go on with you." Her broad smile turned to a frown as Cypher picked at the one piece of dry toast on his plate.

Cypher caught her glance. "Ulcers." His stomach had not caught on to western food; what he wouldn't give for a bowl of his mother's *haleem* about now.

"We'd best be on our way," said the Commodore, dispatching the remainder of his flapjack stack in one bite. "Annie and I will go pack." He pushed himself to a stand with a grunt. "Bring the car around in ten minutes."

Mrs. O'Connor carefully tapped Cypher's shoulder. "I've got just the thing for disagreeable digestion. I won't be a minute." Mrs. O'Connor disappeared into the kitchen.

As Audie mounted the stairs to collect her things, she could hear bottles clinking and pots and pans rattling.

When Mrs. O'Connor returned with a big blue bottle of Dr. Neil's Natural Elixir, she found the dining room completely empty.

Hoisting her skirts, she ran to the door, catching sight of that beautiful touring car gliding away. Oh, well. She patted the apron pocket that held the Commodore's check. He'd paid in full the night before.

A few days later when Mrs. O'Connor attempted to deposit that check, she was presented with some extremely unpleasant news. It was the same news that each of the innkeepers who housed our traveling trio over the next many nights received upon presenting Commodore Crutchfield's checks to *their* banks. Insufficient funds. They say misery loves company. But Mrs. O'Connor didn't realize she had company in her misery at being stiffed for two meals and one night's lodging—and three separate rooms at that! She was particularly suspicious of that chauffeur; perhaps the Commodore was under his spell. She rang up the Sheriff, demanding he take action.

The Sheriff, who had both a bad toothache *and* a newborn, was worthless. All he could think about was getting a good night's sleep. After Mrs. O'Connor went on at some length, he did offer to phone his colleague in the next town over to alert him about the bad check shenanigans. Mrs. O'Connor was so peeved at this lackluster response that she swore never again to donate her orange frosted nut buns for the local law enforcement bake sale.

Audie was unmindful of such events on their travels; eleven-year-olds are not typically well versed in banking practices. Not unlike Mrs. O'Connor, Audie had reasons of her own to be suspicious of the man who called himself Cypher. To be fair, he was always agreeable about mailing postcards for her when they reached a new destination. Yet, she had overheard snippets of secretive telephone conversations each time they bedded down for the night. And once, when they stopped at yet another small-town diner, Cypher begged off lunch, saying he needed some powders for a nasty head-ache. From her seat in the diner, Audie had seen him slip into the Western Union office rather than the drugstore. A puzzling action to be sure.

Audie kept her senses sharp during those days of travel, through Columbus, Zanesville, Uniontown, Frostburg. Her initial hunch had proved correct: They were headed east. She only wished she had been as successful in learning the nature of the mission as she was their direction.

Hagerstown—she read the road sign. "Aren't names fascinating?" she asked aloud. "Do you think the town was named for a Mr. Hager? Or maybe Mrs."

Cypher grunted.

"I commend you for keeping your mind sharp," said the Commodore. "Many a young lass would let hers go as limp as a licorice string on such a journey. But not our Annie."

"I *am* making an effort to keep my mind sharp," Audie admitted. She was pleased with this turn of the conversation. Perhaps it might unlock the secret that the Commodore had held so tightly ever since their departure from Miss Maisie's. "If only I knew what it was I am to be doing when we arrive . . . wherever we arrive . . . I could be of more assistance."

"All in good time, Annie, dear. All in good time." The Commodore tilted his hat over his eyes and assumed his favorite travel activity: sleep.

Well, "all in good time" seemed a step up from his usual, "You do not need to worry your sweet head," or the phrase she'd encountered more often recently, "Children should be seen and not heard."

Audie did her best to temper her impatience. As was pointed out in Professor Helen Moon Ketteman's tome *The People's Proverbs*, "Too many kings can ruin an army." She knew that she must be content with the knowledge that the Commodore was the general and she a mere foot soldier in this undertaking. Whatever it was. But her middle name was Evangeline, not Patience, after all. The Commodore had shown her so many kindnesses on their journey— buying that bag of peppermints in Zanesville, allowing her to order a cherry phosphate with lunch at the diner, and promising her a new wardrobe when they arrived at their destination. If only he knew that the greatest kindness for such a curious girl would be to reveal all about her mission. Alas, it was not to be.

After five days on the road, Cypher nosed the automobile to a stop in front of a shabby hotel on the outskirts of the nation's capital. When Audie, hand on the doorknob to her small hotel room (a placard above her head vowed that George Washington had sojourned there), asked, "Is this our final destination?" the Commodore actually gave a direct answer: "Tomorrow we'll drive into the city. And then our work begins." Audie opened her mouth to inquire further, but he held up his large, be-ringed hand. "Seen, not heard, Annie dear," he reminded her, before closeting himself in his own room. Audie surmised that she could certainly wait a few hours longer for the answer to the question that had plagued her for nearly a week.

She had retired with her books the night before, as had been her habit the entire journey. But, after breakfast, Audie found a newspaper, discarded by another lodger. She picked it up and, hungry for something new, began to read.

"What are you doing?" Cypher snatched the paper from Audie's hands. "Who gave you permission?"

"No one said I couldn't," she answered reasonably.

"You are to assume everything is against orders." He methodically refolded the paper, front page tucked inside.

Audie contemplated working up a tear or two, but such an effort would be wasted on Cypher.

"What's the fuss in here?" The Commodore strode into the room, brushing a bit of tobacco from his otherwise impossibly impeccable white trousers. Audie conjured up a watery glitter in her eyes. On him, tears *might* be effective.

"I only wanted to read the newspaper," she answered, adding a well-placed woebegone hiccup.

"All this racket over reading material?" The Commodore fluffed the outer corners of his moustache. "My dear sir, might I remind you that Miss Smith is my esteemed colleague?"

"Jones," Audie muttered.

Cypher answered the Commodore with a look that Audie could not read. Had Cypher been one to gamble, he might have become a wealthy man playing poker. His face gave little away.

"Here you are, my dear." The Commodore removed the newspaper from Cypher's hands with only the briefest of tussles.

"I admire you for wanting to expand your horizons. Well done. Well done." He handed the neat packet of newsprint to Audie, then turned back to Cypher. "Will you join me in the other room? I would like to go over the plans for tomorrow."

Audie's left ear buzzed as she unfolded the paper. What was it that Cypher had not wanted her to read? She made herself as comfortable as possible on the scratchy horsehair davenport. If she braced one foot against the armrest, she could stay put for several minutes, before sliding to the edge of the seat. She smoothed out the paper, and then studied each page, reading, bracing, sliding. Reading, bracing, sliding.

From the front page of the *Washington Post*, Mr. Henry Ford proclaimed that the automobile would be part of every home, taking its place next to old Dobbin in the family barn. Audie tried to imagine such a thing: wondrous and horrifying at the same time. Wouldn't she love to captain her own automobile? Wouldn't anyone? His fortune had been made dressing up horses and their riders, yet even the Commodore had succumbed to modern pressures to own four-wheeled rather than four-legged transportation. But if everyone drove one, mightn't cities choke on the clouds of gasoline exhaust? At least, old Dobbin's "output" could be put to use, once aged, to help grow vegetables in the garden. The same could not be said of the auto.

Audie read on. Sweet potato profits were up and England was abuzz with war talk, according to other headlines. She flipped pages, pausing briefly when she read, *Whirl of Gayety in Washington Society*. A lengthy sidebar spelled out the rules for the President's upcoming New Year's Day reception: *Persons attending must approach the White House by the west gate, where a line is formed. Upon entering the White House, said line continues in single file through the vestibule, the corridor, and the Red Room to the Blue Room.* And so on and so on. What a lot of blather.

Audie kept reading. Nothing in the remaining pages seemed worthy of Cypher's efforts to keep her from the newspaper. Nor did what she read provide any hint about why the Commodore needed her.

She crumpled the newspaper in her lap. Her current situation was a complete disappointment. Certainly, she'd escaped the drudgery of Miss Maisie's, but to what gain? Six days of bumpy roads and early morning departures from an assortment of second-rate hotels did not, in Audie's mind, qualify as a bona fide adventure. And she had yet to perform the smallest of acts that made a whit of difference in the world.

A wave of disappointment swept over her, causing her to curl up into a ball on the davenport, whose slickery surface unceremoniously dumped her into a rumpled heap on the floor. It was the last thing she'd ever imagined happening, but she found herself longing for Miss Maisie's. Her narrow little cot next to Bimmy, the bedtime stories spun to trundle the triplets off to slumber land, the raisins in the oatmeal. And, not the least, the Punishment Room. Audie ached for Miniver, as well, stalwart cat, who, had she been in the vicinity, would have taken the opportunity to replace the newspaper in Audie's lap.

Audie curled up tighter. She longed for Min so powerfully that she could almost smell her—all dried hay and mouse breath. A deep yearning coursed through Audie's body, eroding every ounce of desire for adventure or good-deed doing. Our distraught heroine had worked herself into such a state, she was certain she could hear Min's distinctive *mer-row*.

Audie pushed herself up with a start.

That was no wishful thinking. That was Min!

Audie rose from the floor and ran to the window, nudging it

ajar a wee bit, admitting entrance to a blast of December's biting breath.

And to a slip of a cat.

"Min!" Audie cried out in her excitement. Then she quieted her voice so as not to alert the men in the other room. "You followed me all this way?" Audie scooped up her feline friend and held her close. "Oh, brave and wonderful cat."

Min wasn't much for fuss. She wriggled out of Audie's grasp and dropped to the floor, nearly soundlessly, then delicately sniffed at the air.

"What am I thinking?" Audie hurried to the breakfast table. "You must be famished." With a bit of egg and bacon and toast from the sideboard, Audie was able to assemble a respectable meal.

"Bees and bonnets," Audie exclaimed as Min tidied herself after dining. "How am I going to keep you out of sight?"

Min stopped in mid-lick of her snowy right paw. Her ears folded back in surprise at Audie's foolish question.

"Oh, what am I saying?" Audie rescued another bacon crumb from the breakfast plates and offered the tidbit. "It'll be like at Miss Maisie's, won't it?" Min removed the bacon from Audie's finger with a tongue as rough as the Commodore's whiskers. Audie sat on the floor, making a nest in her skirt, and there Min perched, purring and warm, while Audie coddled her. "Your timing was perfect," Audie said, nearly confessing to the bout of loneliness that had overtaken her. "A friend makes life so much easier to bear."

A kerfluffle in the next room sent Min darting off Audie's lap. She leapt up onto the davenport, skittering the newspaper to the floor, then bounded across an ornate side table and out the window.

Audie gathered the scattered pages together, returning them to a neat though disordered pile.

"My dear," the Commodore called. "Will you step in here, please?"

Audie stood, moving to place the scrambled newspaper, society pages on top, on the side table. "Coming," she called.

Her eye was caught by a photo she had earlier overlooked. "Dorothy Taft, smiling at her uncle the President." Audie paused after reading the caption. Wouldn't that be a lark, to call the President "uncle"? She tugged on her left earlobe. Glanced again at the photo. Could this Dorothy have something to do with the Commodore's mission? Was that the reason for the buzzing starting anew in her ear?

"Annie!" The Commodore's voice was genial but firm.

Audie glanced at the photo once more, trying to keep her lively imagination reined in. Before she could set the paper down, Cypher marched into the room, and grabbed her arm. For a slim man, he had plump thumbs. "You should come when you're summoned."

Having read through Mrs. Paul's manual sufficient times, Audie's good manners prevented her from pointing out that she was a girl, not a dog. She shook herself from his grasp. "I was merely tidying up." She carefully set the newspaper down, Dorothy's photo on top. As she smoothed the page, she watched Cypher's face for any reaction.

His eyes may have narrowed. Nothing more. "Satisfied?"

"Yes." Audie stood tall, shoulders back. "Quite."

✻ CHAPTER SEVEN ✻

Miss Maisie's Mail

"Don't be impertinent." Miss Maisie rubbed the bridge of her nose, and blinked twice before looking again at Bimmy. The School had been running so much less efficiently since Audacity's departure. Three of the Girls had actually asked for Miss Maisie's help with homework. Cook had left Miss Maisie's Cherry Cordials off the shopping order. Twice. And those triplets had been sniffling so, it was impossible to keep the requisite number of handkerchiefs laundered and pressed. Miss Maisie was going to have to double up on her standing order of headache powders until Audie's return. "What do you mean there is no mail? I saw the postman stop, with my own eyes." She patted her plump palm on the top of the writing desk at which she sat each morning composing notes to the fine ladies of Swayzee, inviting herself to lunch or tea. For some odd reason, she never received replies to any of her missives.

Bimmy's bony shoulders reached upward toward her ears. "I could check again," she offered.

Miss Maisie's eyes squinched. "You're *sure* there was nothing for me?" Mrs. Snidewater had almost smiled at her after services three weeks ago Sunday. Miss Maisie had been expecting an invitation to call on the Snidewaters ever since.

Bimmy's black curls bounced as she nodded vigorously. "Very sure."

The grandfather clock in the entry chimed. "So late already?" Miss Maisie flapped her hand. "Go do something useful. I know! Tell Cook to prepare chocolate pudding for tonight's dessert." She shuddered. "What was she thinking yesterday, serving fresh fruit?"

"Yes, Miss Maisie." Bimmy curtsied and then scurried out of the parlor. The triplets were playing hopscotch on the parquet floor in the old ballroom, to divert themselves while they awaited their turn on the bicycle Miss Maisie had given the girls for Christmas. A single bicycle for seventeen girls meant a lot of waiting one's turn.

Bimmy signaled to her chums and they hopscotched after her, not directly, of course, but following after a discreet pause. Soon all four of them were crammed into their secret hiding place under the rear stairs.

"You have news!" exclaimed Violet. Her sisters pressed their hands over her mouth.

"Shh," said Lavender.

"We don't want Divinity to hear," said Lilac.

Bimmy nodded. "Mum's the word, right?"

Three hands crossed three hearts.

Bimmy reached into her pinafore pocket, a proud smile lighting her dear face. She fanned out a handful of cards bearing postmarks from Columbus, Zanesville, Uniontown, and Frostburg. "We got another." She added the latest postcard to the fan.

"Washington, D.C.," Lilac exclaimed in a low voice.

The girls admired the photograph on the front. "The Ardmore Hotel," Lavender read. "Can you imagine traveling to such a posh place as that?"

The little hidey-hole turned midnight-quiet as four girls stepped outside their circumstances to envision such a possibility. The triplets conjured up images of themselves perched on velveteen-upholstered train seats, noses pressed to the glass as they watched the countryside whiz by, secure in the knowledge that their many trunks—brimming with organza gowns and kid-leather boots and three linen waists apiece—were safely stored in the baggage car.

Bimmy's dream placed her in the locomotive, one leather-gloved hand on the gear handles and one on the whistle. Her arm joggled as if yanking down on the chain to signal far ahead that the train was approaching.

Lilac's imagination was not as vibrant as the others' and her thoughts were quickly back to the situation at hand. "Does this one say anything . . . else?" she whispered.

"Like the others?" Lavender added. In addition to Audie's newsy notes, at the bottom of each prior postcard had been a word or two—SLEPT LIKE A BABY, EATING WELL, IN GOOD SPIRITS—written in a hand strange to all.

"That's what's so odd." Bimmy slowly turned over the latest card, showing the others. "This one's not from Audie a'tall." On the back, in that unfamiliar block print, were written four words.

WISH YOU WERE HERE. Lavender's lips moved as she read them to herself. She smiled. "Of course, she misses us."

"Still, it's an odd thing to write," said Lilac. "How could we be there? We're here. At Miss Maisie's."

"But the point is that she didn't write it, did she?" That realization dawned on Violet's heart-shaped face.

"Is she in trouble, Bimmy?" asked Lilac, a tear of worry coursing down her cheek.

Bimmy's eyes were drawn to the postcard, as if staring at it hard enough would unwrap the cryptic message penciled there. "I don't know. I do not know." She turned the postcard image side up. "But I feel strongly that we must be on full alert for our dear Audie."

CHAPTER EIGHT

A Fashionable Miss

Audie winced as the seamstress poked her a third time with a straight pin.

"Did I nick you, darlin'?" The woman stopped.

"It's nothing, I'm certain." The Commodore shifted in the wicker chair provided for him, drumming his fingers on the arms. "Your concern is most appreciated." He cleared his throat, pulling a watch from his pocket and opening the face. "But we are in a bit of a rush."

The seamstress blushed. "Yes, yes. Sorry, sir." Her fingers became birds, flying over the seams of the navy-blue frock. "There we are." She picked a bit of thread from Audie's shoulder. "You and your daughter can go out for a spot of tea, and by the time you come back, the alterations will be finished."

Audie stole another glance at herself in the mirror. Except for the sash at the hips, this dress was cleanly cut—no ruffles, thank goodness—with a pleated skirt for freedom. It suited Audie fine. The Commodore had decked her out in a completely new wardrobe: two matching dresses, a wool coat with braided trim, leather gloves, a sturdy hat of brown beaver, and a muff. Nothing fancy but everything durable and classic.

"This will be perfect for—" Audie looked at the Commodore. "For?" She had no idea how this new ensemble played into her mission.

The Commodore grunted his way out of the delicate chair. "We'll be back in an hour." He waved Audie off to change back into her Wayward Girl garb. "I'm going to see a man about a horse, my dear." He pulled a cigar from his pocket.

Audie had learned that meant he'd be waiting outside, where he could puff away in peace. "I won't be a minute." She took one last turn in front of the mirror, taking in a girl who no longer looked wayward nor orphaned. The girl attired in navy wool would pass for someone who was going places. Doing things. Of that, there was no doubt. Audie saluted her image and hurried off to change.

* * *

Juice Johnson was the best *Herald* newsboy around. His "read all about its" from the corner of F and Twelfth Streets could grab the ears of gentlemen smack-dab in the middle of the Capitol grounds, blocks and blocks away. At twelve, Juice prided himself on three things: a powerful voice, a curious mind, and spit-shined shoes. Pa—God rest his soul—had taught Juice the secrets of a good shine. "Best foot forward, son. Best foot forward," had been the last words Pa uttered before meeting up with Ma in that heavenly choir. Now Juice lived with his grandfather, W. W. Brown, known to Juice as Daddy Dub.

Not every newsboy could claim a tie to the White House. In fact, not one other newsboy *could* do so. Daddy Dub had been driving presidents since Grant, though he was a bit testy about the sitting president, who preferred engines to horses. "If the good Lord had meant us to ride in such infernal machines, why did He create the equine?" Daddy Dub wondered aloud about a dozen times a day.

Juice would never confess it to his grandfather, but, like President Taft, he himself was smitten with those "infernal machines." Was even saving the odd nickel and dime himself for such a contraption. And when he had one, he would steer it west, as far as that automobile could carry him. Seemed to Juice that the future was not in the nation's capital, but in the nation's fringes. Where the color of a man's skin didn't count for as much as the quality of his actions. West. Seattle was a place that had planted its tendrils in his heart of late. Lots of rain, he heard tell, but couldn't that be handled with a sturdy umbrella? Washington State was a place of tall mountains, deep lakes, and big challenges, and such a landscape called to Juice.

He shifted his bundle to his other shoulder. "Papers! Get your papers!" A handful more sold and he could fetch himself some lunch, a fact that made his belly groan all the louder. The flapjacks Daddy Dub had prepared at dawn were ancient history.

Juice spotted a likely gentleman, decked out in white from head to toe, exiting Garfinkle's Department Store. "Paper, sir?"

"Why, yes, young man." The gentleman flung his white cape over his shoulder, then tossed Juice a dime. "Keep the change."

An eight-cent tip! Juice grinned. The dime fairly glowed in his pocket. Perhaps there was more where this came from.

Juice tipped his cap at the young woman who had also exited the store and was now walking toward the big tipper. "Good day, miss."

The girl cast a quick glance at her companion before returning Juice's smile. "Good day to you, too," she said.

"I don't suppose you could direct us to a café nearby?" The old gent tugged a pocket watch from the vest encircling his ample waist. "For a quick lunch."

"I know just the place." Juice shifted his papers to his other shoulder and pointed. "Up there, a few blocks. The Acorn." His stomach grumbled again at the thought of sustenance. "I can show you the way, if you like."

The girl's face lit up at that suggestion, but her father or uncle or whoever shook his head. "Our car is coming, there."

Juice turned to eyeball the tastiest-looking automobile he'd ever seen. Robin's egg blue. He whistled. "That's some ride," he said. American Motor Company, touring car. He studied automobiles like Daddy Dub studied horses. What he wouldn't give to ride one block in that machine.

The driver, tall and fit, eased out from behind the steering wheel, opening the passenger doors first for the old gent and then for the girl. Juice could not take his eye off the vehicle as it glided away from the curb.

Then he shook his head. He must be hungrier than he realized. Like to be seeing things. He shook again. It couldn't be so, but he swore he saw a striped tail, poking out behind the wicker trunk strapped at the rear of the vehicle. Looked to be keeping time like a metronome. After a third shake of his head, Juice saw nothing but the tail end of that fine automobile disappearing down the street. Clearly, time for a lunch break.

He patted his jingling pocket, and made his way to the Center Market, where he knew a man who made the juiciest roast beef sandwiches in town.

Mmm, mmm, mmm.

∗CHAPTER NINE∗

Heavens to John James Audubon

The prior resident of the White House, Theodore Roosevelt, had been a nature lover. And there was more to that love than the oft-told story of the bear whose life Teddy had supposedly saved. A hunter, yes, but TR appreciated all of God's creatures, great and small, and especially the feathered small. This avid birder once compiled a list of the species, numbering fifty-six, he'd observed on the White House grounds. That list included a pair of saw-whet owls that spent several weeks by the south portico one June.

The current president was more unimaginative in his appreciation of the animal world, an appreciation that focused on, and was limited to, Pauline, the White House cow.

One who did share Roosevelt's esteem of the winged world was at the moment patrolling the estate at Pennsylvania Avenue, though on four feet rather than the presidential pair. At a rustling in a nearby shrub, the feline froze, crouched, and stared intently through the shrub's bare twigs. So still and camouflaged was she that a passerby might not notice her.

As a matter of fact, such a passerby—the man sneaking around the corner of the nearby building—only narrowly missed stepping on the creature's switching tail. By sheer luck, his foot touched the slushy ground just beyond it, averting disaster for both cat and man. Cat, because the injury would've hampered the hunt. Man, because the cat's howl of pain might have alerted others to his presence, a situation he desperately desired to avoid.

Thus the man, who carried the scent of the desert about him, pussyfooted onward to his destination, pausing only briefly at the sound of a twiggy tussle. Intent on his mission, he did not see the cat slink off under a stand of Katherine crab apple trees, bearing the lifeless body of a snowbird in her mouth. With quiet crunching, the cat consumed her supper, adding the tiny feathers to a slowly growing pile at the base of her favorite tree. Since taking up residence in Washington, D.C., the cat had reduced the President's Park avian population by several dozen. Nature, though beautiful, is not always kind.

Seeing neither cat nor danger, the man continued on *his* way, knocking discreetly—*shave and a haircut, two bits*—at a door near the rear of the great house. This was all done per instructions received from a member of the Secret Service. You may well wonder how it was that a man from the desert established contact with an officer of the presidential police force. There are many secrets in the White House. Some that may never be divulged. Here, we may share one bit of information: Several months prior, the man from the desert, carrying a letter of commendation from the Shah of

Persia, had applied for a position on the White House police force. Narrower minds could not look past the color of the man's skin. But one officer took note of his demeanor and his record and gave the man a card printed with his telephone number. Direct line. We may say no more about that—matters of national security, etcetera. Regardless, after rapping out the secret knock, the man from the desert was quickly admitted, and as quickly disappeared inside.

After a bit more than a quarter of an hour, as quietly and stealthily as he had entered, the man exited the building. Once again, he passed the cat, ignorant of her presence. She, clever cat, noted his. She watched him glance nervously over his shoulder, then break into a loping pace across the grounds and off in the general direction of F Street, where, it may be noted, sat a hotel named Ardmore.

The cat was in no hurry to follow. With the uncanny intuition belonging to all of her kind, she had already surmised the man's destination. Meal completed, she began to tidy herself up, intent on making herself presentable for company.

When she was completely satisfied with her efforts, the cat padded diagonally across the snow-blanketed lawn on four creamy-white paws to pay a call on a friend lodging at the Ardmore Hotel.

CHAPTER TEN

Life in the Lap of Luxury

It wasn't that the bed was uncomfortable. Besides, Audie was accustomed to a lack of nocturnal comfort: The mattresses at Miss Maisie's were more lumps than filling. It wasn't that Audie's sixth-floor room was too cool or too warm. Nor was it too noisy. The Commodore could be snoring away across the hall—no doubt he was—but Audie was not troubled by one rumble. It was quiet enough to successfully eavesdrop on Cypher's low-toned telephone conversations, had he, too, been on the sixth floor. As was proper for a chauffeur, though, he had been assigned to a room on the servants' floor. Everything about the Ardmore Hotel was exactly as advertised: "meeting the modern traveler's comforts with old-fashioned care."

One such comfort was a watchful eye over Audie at night. At the hotel's insistence, the Commodore had hired a petite French maid, her apron as crisp as a potato chip, who was now asleep on a cot in Audie's sitting room. Audie hadn't yet learned the maid's name; their only conversation had been the maid's whispered, *"Bonne nuit, ma chérie."*

The hotel was so quiet, Audie could hear the maid talking in her sleep. If only Audie had been more diligent in reading that *Conversational French* book, she might now be able to decipher what the maid was murmuring. Whatever it was, it sounded ever so cheerful. French was such a musical tongue!

Audie had every reason to be cheerful herself: ensconced in this luxurious hotel. A double bed all to herself. The promise of room service breakfast, wheeled in on a silver cart. Two brand-new look-alike dresses in the armoire across the room, in a style which made Audie feel like a model on the cover of *The Ladies' Home Journal*. A pair of black Mary Janes, with the strap buttoning at the middle of her foot—"the smartest style," according to the salesclerk at Behrends'—were lined up in the bottom of the armoire, next to her new boots and right under the cheviot-wool coat with the stylish trim. Most girls would be supremely content with such comfort, food, and fashion.

But Audie was not most girls. She had padded over to the hotel room door to double check. Yes, each lock was locked. And the security chain was firmly drawn. She had left the window ajar for some fresh air, but it was the sixth floor after all: perfectly safe. Perhaps it had been unwise to have that second ice cream sundae after supper. Audie couldn't imagine what else might be keeping her from slumber.

Had the maid been awake and had she been fluent in English, *she* would have suggested that it was not the wisest course of action for a girl with Audie's imagination to read from Detective P. Gardella's book, *Fair Criminals, Foul Minds*, directly before retiring for the night. But the maid was merrily conversing in her sleep, so gave no such suggestion. And the very book in question was resting once again on Audie's knees.

She flipped past the chapters on bunco men and swindlers, having already read those. Twice. She found herself immersed in the chapter entitled "Friend or Foe?" These words jumped off the page in the lamplight's glow: *People of respectability and inexperience, who have no knowledge of the criminal classes, usually imagine that every criminal is a hardened villain, incapable of even the ordinary feelings of family affection, and that of necessity the professional crook, thief, or burglar is uneducated and ignorant. In fact, nothing could be further from the truth. Do you see that well-dressed, respectable-looking man glancing over the editorial page of the* Sun? *You would be surprised to know that he is a professional burglar and that he has a loving wife and a family of children who little know the "business" which takes him away for many days and nights at a time . . . As a matter of fact, some of the brightest brains and keenest minds belong to professional criminals. They live by their wits and must need keep those wits sharp and active.*

Audie looked up from the page, pondering the author's admonition. It was true: If she had been asked to describe a criminal, she would've described someone rough and sly and slovenly. Thanks to Detective Gardella's guidance, Audie now realized that such an appearance would cause a stir in a crowd of respectable folk. And respectable folk were exactly the kind targeted by the criminal element.

She leaned against the down-filled bed pillow, and cast herself back to this afternoon, and their entrance into the hotel lobby. Audie recalled seeing a distinguished-looking gent reading the *Washington Post* in one of the club chairs under a poster advertising

Circus Kardos, near the reception desk. Could he be someone leading a double life? A cat burglar perhaps? And what about the flash of red, jaunty in that young mother's extraordinary *chapeau*? Would a modern matriarch wear such an attention-attracting feather? Could that have been a signal to an accomplice in some complex and mercenary scheme?

Detective Gardella's book had opened Audie's eyes to the fact that danger lurked everywhere. Well, everywhere but back home in Swayzee, where the most untoward event of recent history had occurred when the ancient Mrs. Horst Van Beeker picked a generous bouquet of her neighbor's prize tulips. Mrs. Van Beeker had imagined herself a young girl again, back in the Netherlands, selected to present flowers to Grand Duchess Sophie for May Day. The neighbor had shrieked and carried on, but after Mr. Van Beeker paid for the damages, that was the end of that.

A scrabbling at the windowsill redirected Audie's attention. How Min had managed to find her, here at the Ardmore, was one of the eight wonders of the world. Audie smiled. And climbing up to this very window from the street six floors below constituted the ninth wonder. One for each of Min's charmed lives.

"Hey, puss," Audie whispered, kicking back the bedcovers and opening the nightstand drawer. "What do you think of this for a bedtime snack?" She held out a bit of buttered biscuit, a sliver of ham, and a chunk of cheese, spirited off the supper table and into Audie's pocket.

Min delicately sniffed the offering, but declined to partake.

"What—not good enough for you?" Audie rolled to the edge of the mattress to set the banquet on the floor. "Or not hungry?" She suspected the latter but refused to think about the creature that might have given its life to sate Min's appetite.

"What's it like out there?" The day had been a hustle-bustle of moving lodgings, shopping for new clothes, and so forth. Audie had yet to see much of the nation's capital. "Is it beautiful?"

Min answered with a flick of her elegant tail. *A cat finds scarce beauty in concrete and marble and monuments.*

Audie slid over in the bed, patting the coverlet. "Come sit with me."

Min considered the invitation. After a respectable pause—so as not to appear overeager—she leapt, landing smack-dab on the book Audie had been reading. It slid to the floor with a thunk.

"Are you all right, mademoiselle?" a sleepy voice called from the next room.

"Yes! *Oui!*" Audie picked the book up and returned it to her lap. "Min, you have to be more careful," she whispered.

Min considered that warning while she cleaned between her back toes.

"Bees and bonnets, you lost my place." The book was now flipped open to an illustration of a man's hand. Audie glanced at the caption beneath. *The ordinary criminal's hand has a peculiarly rough shape, with the thumb being very plump and short. The small finger is turned inward, and bluntness is the hand's chief characteristic.*

Her breath caught in her throat. She reread the words. Why, this described Cypher's hand to a tee! She slapped the book shut, throwing her arms around Min's neck. She pressed close to one furry ear and murmured, "Thank you, dear friend." She should have tumbled to this much sooner. What upstanding citizen would call himself Cypher, anyway? The word itself implied secrets.

She must warn the Commodore. But this was delicate business. It was he who had hired Cypher, entrusting him with his current duties. Audie did not know their shared history. Had she been aware that Cypher had entered the Commodore's employ mere hours before their appearance at Miss Maisie's, she might have been less hesitant to share her misgivings. Without that knowledge, our heroine perceived that the Commodore might not be receptive to one mere piece of evidence of Cypher's criminality.

Audie hopped out of bed, quietly opening the desk drawer to remove a sheet of hotel stationery and a pencil. She settled herself on the desk chair, licked the end of the pencil, and began a list, starting with the description of the common criminal's hand. Reflecting back on their journey, she wrote down every action that had niggled at her at the time, but that she had discounted. All those late-night murmured phone calls. The Western Union incident. The fuss over her reading the newspaper the previous morning.

Audie stopped writing mid-word as a notion struck her. Every time she had asked the Commodore about the mission they were undertaking, Cypher had been present. Ears tuned in to their every word. What if the Commodore had been hesitant all this time to reveal his plan because he shared her reservations?

He had hired the man; he must be at a loss in his predicament. And ever watchful because of it. How could she have been so oblivious? There was no other conclusion that Audie could draw than the fact that the Commodore was not trying to keep information from *her* but from Cypher.

All the more reason to show the Commodore her list.

CHAPTER ELEVEN

A Fox in the Henhouse

"Here you are, miss." The smartly uniformed elevator operator, smiling brightly, safely delivered Audie to the lobby. She smiled back, stepping out onto the marble floor, her new gray kid boots with red buttons tip-tapping in a most dignified way. These new boots had ample room for her toes—and her two gold coins.

The Commodore was in conference with a bellman as she approached. She hurried over, standing off to one side, not wanting to intrude on the conversation, but close enough to hear the Commodore grumble, "But you agreed to twenty-five." The bellman caught sight of Audie, shook his head, and said, in a voice loud enough for Audie to hear, "Shall I call you a cab, sir?"

"Cab?" The Commodore sounded confused, then he, too, noticed Audie. "Good morning, my dear." The Commodore's face lit up in a smile. "Did you sleep well?"

"Yes, thank you." Audie straightened her hat. "Are we eating breakfast here?" She looked around the lobby. "Where's Cypher?"

Maybe this was her chance to speak to the Commodore. She felt in her coat pocket for the list she'd made the night before.

The Commodore waved his hand. "Gave him the day off." He turned to the bellman. "You may call me a taxi now."

"There's something I need to tell you." Audie slid the list out of her pocket as the bellman stepped out into the slush to whistle down a cab.

"Not now, Annie. My mind's awhirl." The Commodore checked his pocket watch. "You have a nice breakfast in your room. We'll talk later."

A cab pulled up and the bellman held the door open. "But this is important." Audie squeezed around the Commodore and slid into the cab.

"Where to?" the cabbie asked.

"What?" The Commodore tugged at his cravat. "Nowhere."

"You don't need a cab?"

"Yes. I need a cab." The Commodore motioned energetically. "Come out, my dear. I have a business meeting."

Audie pressed herself against the far side of the door. "I won't get out. Not until you listen to me."

The Commodore glanced at his pocket watch again, then groaned. If he was late to the station, he would never hear the end of it from Elva.

"All right." He slid into the back seat. The bellman tapped the taxi roof to give the signal to go, casting an odd look at Audie as he did so. She shivered.

The Commodore picked up a blanket from the seat next to him and tucked it over their legs. "We'll breakfast soon. After . . .

afterward." Elva would have conniptions if he threw a wrench in the plans this early in the game. He was going to have to ditch Annie at the station.

The Commodore leaned his head back on the seat. It had been years since he'd seen Elva Finch, though he had been her most faithful pen pal while she'd been in prison. He had been shocked to hear from her, poor thing, but she'd quickly explained how she'd been framed and it wasn't one bit her fault that her boss had left all that loose money sitting around. Besides, she had only intended to borrow it.

The Commodore had no choice but to believe in her innocence; after all, it was Elva who'd helped launch Crutchfield Creations all those years ago, when the rosette order for the Swayzee Independence Day celebration had failed to arrive. They were only high schoolers, but she'd pitched in, sitting up all night with the Commodore until there were sufficient beribboned decorations for every steed in town. That was the day that Crutchfield Creations came into being. All those boys who'd laughed at the Commodore for his talents at darning and knitting, rather than baseball, quickly changed their tune when they came to him, hats in hand, looking for a job.

He sighed at that memory, then fumbled in his pocket. "I've been meaning to give you a little pin money." He held out a handful of coins. Perhaps he could send Annie off to buy something to eat once they arrived. It was imperative that she and Elva not meet until the appointed hour.

"But I need to tell you something important—" Audie pressed her point. "About Cypher."

The Commodore tut-tutted. "I know he's rather stern. But he's not a bad sort once you get to know him. Why, I saw him post a card to his mother the other day." He jingled the coins in his hand. "Put these in your pocket."

She took the coins. "That's just it! He *is* bad." Audie had her list out, ready to read it aloud.

"Annie, dear thing." The Commodore pinched the bridge of his nose between his thumb and forefinger. "I was up rather late last night. Arranging . . . things. I must ask that you be a good girl now. Seen and not heard, and all that." As if to close the conversation, he closed his eyes and leaned his head back.

"But—"

"Shh!" With eyes shut, he raised a finger to his lips. "I must have some peace and quiet."

Audie exhaled loudly, then shoved the list and the coins in her pocket. She glared out the window as they motored along F Street. At Judiciary Square, Audie began to feel a bit queasy. At first she thought it was due to frustration, but her stomach let her know otherwise. It needed nourishment. She pressed on its emptiness. A quick left on New Jersey and then a sharp right put the car on Massachusetts, and Audie's innards were in an even worse state. She could hardly enjoy the sight of the magnificent Union Depot looming in front of them, a giant white beehive, abuzz with travelers instead of bees. The comings and goings only made her queasier.

"Here we are." The Commodore puffed his way out of the backseat.

Audie swallowed, then followed. A wave of dizziness swept over her as she stepped to the curb. She braced herself against the taxi door.

"Perhaps you should return to the hotel," the Commodore suggested, clearly picking up on his young companion's physical distress. "I will meet you there later." Annie had no idea but Elva Finch in a state was something one desired to avoid at all costs. That the Commodore knew too well from experience. He could not afford to be late in meeting her train. And he absolutely could not show up with Annie in tow.

Legs aquiver, Audie supported herself on the cab door. She intended to follow the Commodore, but his strides were too long and purposeful, and before she knew it, she was in a heap on the cold, damp ground, trouser legs and skirts bustling around her. The cab was nowhere to be seen.

After a bit, she sat up, pulling her knees to her chest, tucking her skirts around her legs. She leaned her head forward. When the light-headedness had passed, she looked up and into a pair of concerned brown eyes.

"You feeling punk?" The boy shifted the sheaf of newspapers on his shoulder.

Audie shook her head. "I didn't get breakfast."

The boy nodded, smiling. "I miss a meal, I 'bout fall down myself. I know a place you can get yourself a bite." He held his free hand out to her.

"Well, I—" She should probably look for the Commodore. But where to begin? There were so many people! He had disappeared like the proverbial needle in a haystack. And she was so hungry!

Audie felt certain that agreeing to this boy's suggestion would violate nearly every rule in *Mrs. Paul's Manners for the Modern Young Lady*, but there was something so solid and true in his eyes. Something she could trust. She took the boy's hand. "Thank you for your kindness to a stranger."

"Oh, we're not strangers," he said. "I saw you yesterday."

Audie nodded in recognition. "That's right. You sold the—my uncle—a paper." As she wobbled to a stand, she introduced herself.

"Pleased to meet you, Audacity. I'm Juice." He pushed his way through the crowds, clearing a path for her. Audie held tight to his sleeve. She wasn't about to lose her benefactor. Soon they were in front of a food stall with a rough wooden sign nailed above it: LULU's. Juice ordered her a "Lulu's special with a cup of joe." Audie had never tasted anything so delicious: The "special" was a pastry filled with some kind of spiced meat. "Joe" was hot coffee.

She reached into her pocket for additional coins. "May I have two more, please?" When the food vendor handed over the pair of packets, she gave one to Juice. "A small reward for rescuing me," she said. With two filling pasties consoling her stomach and the hot coffee warming her bones, she felt ready to face her situation.

"I was with my uncle," she said. Though Juice seemed infinitely trustworthy, this was not the time to reveal all of the morning's events and concerns. "And when I felt unwell, I lost him in the crowd."

"Well, he shouldn't be too hard to find, all in white like that," Juice observed. "Tell you what. You rest on that bench there, finish your coffee. I'll go scout around, see if I can see him. If I do, I'll bring him here."

"Oh, I couldn't ask you to do that."

"Sure you could." He winked. "Figure finding you should be worth at least another dime." His chuckle warmed the air like the aroma of fresh-baked buttermilk biscuits. "Now, don't you go away."

Audie had no intention of going anywhere. She had a map of the city in her trusty *Nethery's Atlas*, but hadn't yet had the opportunity to memorize it. The idea of getting herself lost was most unappealing. She did take a few baby steps from the bench to avail herself of a nearby mailbox. But after she posted a card to the Girls back at Miss Maisie's, it was right back to the spot where Juice had left her.

Juice, in the meantime, had dived back into the throngs in front of the depot. Audie's knight in shining armor quickly scouted the perimeter of the plaza in front of the Depot, deftly dodging automobiles and horse-drawn carriages. The few glimpses of white he'd caught so far all proved to be false alarms. Juice moved across the plaza, toward the station's grand entrance. Wait—there. Was that him? There with the lady who looked like some kind of oversized bird?

Juice veered around an elderly couple, two nannies pushing prams, and a gaggle of giggling young ladies, daintily high-stepping through the slush in their fine boots. He was mere yards away from his target, about to raise his arm, to call out a greeting, when something he witnessed stopped him in his tracks.

Had Juice not been forced to spend several weeks with a shady cousin after Pa's death, before Daddy Dub found him, Juice would not have comprehended the unfolding scene. To the untrained eye, it would appear that the large birdlike woman with Audacity's uncle had been nudged into that skinny gent by the teeming crowds. Ah, but Juice knew better. He observed apologies offered and accepted and watched as the pair of strangers once again went on their appointed ways.

If Juice was right—oh, he was so painfully sorry to think that he was—then Audacity's uncle's female friend was walking off richer by that businessman's wallet and pocket watch. At the very least.

He turned away, sickened. Audacity seemed like a solid sort. A good egg. Not the type to be part of bamfoozlement such as what he'd that moment observed. Juice reflected on his time with his cousin; perhaps Audacity was stuck in the same carriage he'd been, forced to participate in something unseemly. Or perhaps she had no part of such a scalliwag's trade, and was completely ignorant of it.

Juice sold a few more papers while he pondered his options. When he saw Audacity's uncle and the woman slide into a taxi, driving off without a backward glance or apparent thought about a misplaced young girl, his decision was made.

He would escort his new friend back to her hotel, by way of the White House stables. Daddy Dub was as keen a reader of people as he was of horseflesh. If he sensed anything false in Audacity, Juice would leave her and her uncle to their reprehensible ways.

But if Daddy Dub took her measure and found it admirable, that would be a horse of a different color. That would mean Audacity was in trouble with no one in this big city but Juice to watch out for her safety.

And watch Juice would.

CHAPTER TWELVE

Postcard from the Nation's Capital

Mr. Scattergood had scarcely finished slapping the reins against Jewell's back before Bimmy ran out to see what he'd deposited in the faded red mailbox. As the postman and his chestnut horse and carriage jostled away down the lane, Bimmy snatched out the mail, sorting it into two piles. The handful of bills for Miss Maisie would be delivered to the parlor. But one item from the box was slipped straight into Bimmy's pinafore pocket.

After the day's lessons from Professor Teachtest, made excruciatingly unbearable without Audie to liven them up, Bimmy and the triplets excused themselves from a rousing session of snipping paper dolls from the Sears, Roebuck and Co. catalog (Divinity always picked the best pages for herself anyway) and met up under the stairway.

"I saw the postman stop at our box," Violet reported.

"Is there news?" Lavender asked breathlessly.

"I miss Audie," Lilac confessed, unable to keep a tear of longing from trickling down her fair cheek. Her sisters began to sniffle, too.

"Shh!" Bimmy cautioned, waving her hands at the trio. "We don't want anyone to hear us." She did her best to imitate Audie and, after a short delay, was able to calm the triplets and dry their tears. Once they were quiet, Bimmy removed an object from her pocket.

"Another postcard!" Three blonde heads touched as the girls bent over the dispatch, eager to feel some connection to their absent friend.

"The Washington Monument!" exclaimed Lavender.

"It's so tall," added Lilac.

"I wonder if she climbed to the top," said Violet. "I would."

"Me too," said Bimmy.

Lilac shivered. "Oh, not me. Too frightening." She clasped her sister's hand. "Promise you won't."

Violet laughed. "That's an easy promise to make. How would we four ever manage a journey to the nation's capital?"

Lavender nodded, but Lilac bit her lip. "Well, Audie did it," she pointed out reasonably.

"But *we* are not Audie," said Bimmy. And that truthful observation seemed to satisfy the youngest of the triplets.

"I wonder what other sights she's seen," Lavender asked.

"Maybe she's written about them." Bimmy flipped the card over to read the message there in their beloved companion's hand. "'I can only imagine how lovely it will be here in the spring,'" Audie had written. Bimmy stumbled over a few of the words; though Bimmy was loathe to speak of it, Audie's penmanship was the one area of her life that needed a great deal of work. "'Nearly two thousand cherry trees—a gift from Japan—will form a miles-long parade of pink-blossomed soldiers, standing at attention along the avenue. I have yet to learn what my duties are to be here, but there may be more to them than meets the eye. Out of room. Love to all. Audacity Jones.'"

"Oh, she writes so well," sighed Lavender. "I can almost see those cherry trees."

"I can smell them!" added Lilac.

Violet and Bimmy did not make comment, but traded glances.

"What?" Lilac, ever sensitive, caught the exchange.

"What?" Lavender was completely lost. "Cherry trees."

"Violet, you think something's wrong," Lilac pushed her sister to confide in them. Violet reluctantly traced her finger over Audie's signature. Bimmy sighed. "That's exactly my worry, too."

"I don't understand," exclaimed Lilac.

"Me either," said Lavender.

Bimmy took the postcard and pointed to the address, reading it aloud: "To Bimmy, Lavender, Lilac, and Violet, care of Miss Maisie's School for Wayward Girls."

"That's us. That's our correct address," Lilac said.

"Otherwise it wouldn't have reached us," Lavender added.

"But the postcard is to us. Us." Bimmy pressed the card to her chest. "Do we ever call her Audacity?"

After a heartbeat, three blonde heads shook in unison.

"Something is afoot and I believe Audie is endeavoring to send us a message." Bimmy exhaled deeply. Audie's whispered words of parting now batted at Bimmy's memory like a moth at lamplight:

"There are answers in the Punishment Room." She dared not yet share these words with her companions.

"We may be called upon to test our mettle," Bimmy said solemnly. "But we will do it. For Audie's sake."

"For Audie's sake," the triplets repeated, trembling.

They remained in their hidey-hole under the stairs until the supper gong. Remained there without saying one more word.

CHAPTER THIRTEEN

Finches and Horseflesh

"I tell you, there is a cat in here!" Elva Finch sneezed three more times. She tugged a floral handkerchief from her handbag and held it to her nose as she paced around the room. "A filthy, disgusting, flea-bitten cat."

"In a hotel?" The Commodore chuckled. "That seems highly unlikely, my dear."

By way of disagreement, Elva Finch sneezed yet again. "My eyes are going to swell completely shut. And then how will I cook that soup?"

"Let me open the window." The Commodore started across the room.

"You dolt—it's freezing out there. And I had to hock my fur for that train ticket." Elva flourished her handkerchief in front of her face, sending her signature scent of gardenias wafting toward the Commodore. Now he sneezed.

Elva perched on the arm of the plushest of the room's two chairs. "I'm starved, too."

"I have made luncheon arrangements." The Commodore ran his fingers across his moustache as if to reassure himself it was still attached beneath his nose. "But—"

"You are buying, aren't you, Stinky?"

Elva's glare loosened something in the Commodore's bowels. He sat, too. Abruptly.

"Of course. Of course. And don't call me that." The Commodore detested that schoolyard nickname, bestowed upon him for reasons we'll not go into here. "It's Commodore Crutchfield now."

Elva Finch merely raised one eyebrow in response. "Fine. What about lunch, *Commodore*?"

"I was only hesitating because young Annie has not returned." For the first time since concocting his plan, the Commodore was beset by doubts. Who would've imagined that orphan being such a nuisance, getting lost like this? And how was it that he had forgotten what Elva could be like when she was in one of her tempers? *He* had wanted to search for Annie but Elva had put her foot down. Thank goodness their partnership was to be short-lived; in a bit more than twenty-four hours, he'd be steaming his way to Venezuela. He had no idea what Elva's plans entailed. And he didn't want to know.

"Well, you said she's twelve, didn't you? As I told you at the station: A girl that age can certainly find her way home." Elva sniffed, testing a sneeze.

"She might be eleven." He really couldn't remember. But she was a spunky little thing, wasn't she? Speaking up like that at the orphanage, full of substance and verve? A child like that could certainly find her way to the Ardmore. The more the Commodore considered the facts, the more he was certain that Elva was on the nose in assessing Annie's abilities.

"And if she can't find her way back . . . well, she's an orphan. She should be used to such disappointments. And we can always find another." Elva pulled an enormous downy puff from her handbag and began to powder her impressive nose.

The Commodore quailed. He had been uneasy about Elva's request for an orphan from the get-go. "We don't want anyone with connections," she had said. He had to agree that part of the plan made sense. But the rest. He hadn't been sure. And was much less sure now. It had been bad enough finding *one* orphan. He dreaded the thought of having to track down another. Besides, he'd grown rather fond of this particular orphan. Annie had taught him to play Twenty Questions, which had made the long car trip east more bearable. She complimented his singing voice—was especially fond of his rendition of "Go Tell Aunt Rhody"—and never minded sharing her dessert. Yes, he had to admit, little Annie had worn a soft spot into his heart. He would miss her when they went their separate ways. Assuming she turned up.

"Well, my dear. Your earlier point is well taken. Annie is indubitably capable of retracing her steps to the hotel." The Commodore patted his middle. "In all the excitement of meeting you at the train, I forgot to breakfast myself." He pushed himself to a stand. "I've made a reservation at the Delmont Café. A mere hop, skip, and a jump from here."

Elva Finch launched off the chair arm and drew herself up to her full height. "Then the taxi fare won't be too dear, will it?"

The Commodore sighed deeply. Women were entirely too much

bother, no matter what their age. Successfully masking his irritation, he offered his arm to his guest. "Shall we go?"

Occupied by their leave-taking, neither Elva nor the Commodore noticed a movement behind the window drapes. As the door clicked shut behind them, a loyal tabby removed herself from her hiding spot and patrolled the room with purpose. Before she'd been overcome by a sneezing fit, Elva Finch had been unpacking her bags. Min nosed aside a letter postmarked Paris, from a Monsieur and Madame LeGarde thanking Mrs. Finch for finding them a daughter. The cat pawed through stacks of neatly folded garments, stopping to sniff a cook's uniform tucked away under two corsets, three pairs of muslin bloomers, and a percale housedress in an especially hideous paisley print.

Min had no way of knowing that this particular cook's uniform—obtained through a shady exchange—was issued only to women working for Isabella Woodard, whose exclusive Ladies Exchange provided help for all the best homes in the District of Columbia. And one of those homes happened to be that of President Taft and the First Lady. A president with a fondness for Terrapin Soup. (We are horrified at this detail as well you might be. The broth is such an unpleasantly turtley shade of green, and one must take care to remove all of the reptilian scales. And then there is the problem of what to do with the shells. But who are we to question the gustatory preferences of a president?) And Mrs. Taft believed that only English cooks were capable of preparing the dish satisfactorily. Ergo, she frequently telephoned the irreproachable Mrs. Woodard to hire said English cook to prepare said Terrapin Soup. And, coincidentally, this was a dish planned for the New Year's Eve menu the very next night.

Min did not know that, not any of it. But she did know that something about the uniform smelled fishy. And not in a good way.

* * *

Juice led Audie through the spotless stables, past one empty stall after another.

"Where are all the horses?" Audie asked.

A voice from behind her spat out the answer: "It's those con-sarned automobubbles."

"Aw, Daddy Dub." Juice shook his head as an older man, resembling an oak leaf in late autumn, all brown and crinkly, hobbled toward them. "Times change."

The old man squinted at Juice, jerking his head toward the White House. "Only one in that whole place I got any respect for is that nice Miz Jaffray. She won't have nuthin' to do with those awful things, either. I drive her to the market every week, sometimes twice, all proper. A brougham in the winter, and an open carriage come summer." He nodded toward a pair of stalls across the way. "With Murphy and Selma in charge."

Selma looked a little testy, but Murphy had such beautiful melted chocolate eyes that Audie couldn't help asking if she might pet him.

"He's my astronomer." Daddy Dub grinned.

Audie stroked the horse's long muzzle, running her hand down a long swath of coarse hair that ended at his velvety nose. Murphy snuffled, wrinkling his lips against her palm, searching for a bit of carrot or apple or sugar. "Astronomer?"

"Always got his head up in the sky." Daddy Dub tapped Juice on the arm. "Like this grandson of mine here. Only I suspect Murphy's dreaming of a nice big pasture somewheres and this one dreams of those infernal machines. And getting far away from this old man and this old city."

Juice ducked his head. "I like it here fine," he said.

"That's why you're counting the days till you're old enough to leave." Daddy Dub snorted. "Wants to go west, of all things."

"Audacity didn't come here to listen to a family squabble." Juice broke a clean piece of straw from a hay bale, put it in his mouth, and chewed energetically.

"That's some kind of name," Daddy Dub commented.

"Thank you," Audie answered, though she wasn't certain she'd been paid a compliment.

Juice's grandfather looked her up and down. It was only a quick glance, but there was something in it that made Audie feel like a horse being checked out by a potential buyer. Then Daddy Dub picked up a bridle and turned it over in his hands. "You shoulda seen this place when Mr. Roosevelt was in charge. Had so many horses, we had to rent stables nearby." He picked up a bottle of neat's-foot oil and a rag and began to rub.

"That stall over there belonged to Diamond, the president's old polo pony. Big black baby, was Diamond. All the Roosevelt children learned to ride on him." Daddy Dub rubbed more vigorously, warming to his topic. "Little Archie's pony, Algonquin—where was that pony from?"

"Iceland," Juice said. "He was an Icelandic pony."

"Right. Sweet little calico. Though Mrs. Roosevelt didn't think it any too sweet when those boys rode him right up into the White House." Daddy Dub sucked between his teeth. "And didn't those horses look sharp all decked out in Mr. Roosevelt's blue? Rosettes on the bridles, on the footmen's hats. It was a sight to see."

"Cockades," said Audie.

"Pardon?" Daddy Dub stopped in mid-rub.

"Someone told me they're called cockades." She shook her head. "It doesn't matter."

"Yessir, those were some salubrious times. Salubrious times." Daddy Dub's laugh faded and he shook his head sadly. "Guess it don't pay to long for what's good and gone."

Audie looked around the quiet stable. Each empty stall must be like a hole in Daddy Dub's heart. "When you described it, I could almost see the way it was. It must have been breathtaking. The horses all decked out. You all decked out." She smiled and Daddy Dub stopped fussing with the bridle to smile back.

"How'd you meet this no-good grandson of mine?" he asked.

Audie gave Murphy's muzzle another pat. "Oh, he was my knight in shining armor at the train station."

"She got separated from her uncle," Juice clarified.

Audie stared at her boots. She hated to mislead Juice. And Daddy Dub.

"Uh-huh. You don't say." Daddy Dub set the bridle down and stepped over to a sink to scrub the oil off his hands. "You two come on back to my office. We'll have some tea."

* * *

Tea was served with thick slices of gingerbread and lively conversation. Daddy Dub regaled Audie with stories of each of the past presidents he'd driven for. "One time, President Grant had to have this particular horse. Absolutely had to have it. Paid six hundred dollars for the nag, the durned fool."

"The horse wasn't worth it?" Audie asked.

"Horse was worth twice that!" Daddy Dub laughed. "Finest horse I ever did see. But Grant couldn't rub two nickels together. President of the U-Nited States and he needed every cent of his salary to make ends meet." Daddy Dub shook his head. "This is some kind of country, I tell you." He laughed again, then took another puff on his pipe.

Somewhere in the distance, Audie heard a clock chime one. "Oh, dear! The time. I'd better get to the hotel. The C—I mean, my uncle, will be so worried." She jumped up, brushing crumbs from her skirt.

"I'll escort you," Juice offered.

Juice was not as chatty as his grandfather, but the walk back passed pleasantly and they were soon in front of the Ardmore.

"Well, thank you for everything!" Audie stuck out her hand. Juice shook.

"There you are, Annie!" The Commodore barreled out of the hotel, inserting himself between Audie and Juice, grabbing her arm. "I've been frantic. Come along. Come along."

As she was tugged inside, Audie cast a backward glance at Juice. His eyes did not say *good-bye* but *see you soon.*

* * *

After supper that night, when Daddy Dub had lit his pipe and Juice had polished off a third piece of Mrs. Jaffray's mincemeat pie, they warmed themselves in front of the potbelly stove in their small rooms at the back of the stables. Daddy Dub used to live in the White House basement, in rooms off the kitchens, like the other help, but once President Taft reduced the number of horses, Daddy Dub moved to the stables. "All kinds of space to stretch out now," he had explained to Mrs. Jaffray. "I can do my chores without anyone pestering me." He'd winked at the housekeeper. "Could hide out for days without anyone turning up to put me to work." Mrs. Jaffray and Daddy Dub had shared a good laugh. Everybody at the White House knew that Daddy Dub put in more effort than most men half his age.

Full from supper, Juice poked around in the stove, stirring up the embers to add another chunk of wood. He fussed with the fire while he sorted out how to ask Daddy Dub's opinion of Audie without giving away his own fears.

"You going to mash that flame right out?" Daddy Dub shook tobacco from a pouch into the bowl of his pipe and tamped it down. "Because these old bones prefer to be warm."

Juice leaned the poker against the fireplace. "I was just thinking," he began.

The old man lit his pipe, shaking the wooden match to extinguish the flame. "'Bout that little gal you brought 'round today?"

Juice had long ago stopped being surprised by his grandfather's intuition. He nodded.

"You didn't find her any too soon." Daddy Dub took three puffs on his pipe.

Juice picked up a stick of cordwood. "What do you mean?"

"She's going to need our help." He tapped his pipe on the ashtray.

"Pretty darned quick, too, 'cording to my rheumatiz. Best to keep an eye on her."

Juice managed to load the wood into the stove without dropping it. How did Daddy Dub know such things? That was a mystery.

But it was no mystery that he was rarely ever wrong.

CHAPTER FOURTEEN

A Friend in Deed

From her perch on the ledge outside a certain sixth-floor room at the Ardmore Hotel, the cat washed her paws after her evening meal. The many members of the Capital Audubon Society would've been heartsick had they known to what degree the avian population had dwindled since the cat's arrival in their fair city. But the hotel staff was pleased to find fewer and fewer signs of mice in the kitchen pantries and service hallways.

The cat, being a cat, was unconcerned about the opinions of either group of humans. Cats, on the whole, find most bipeds extraordinarily dull. But this particular cat was rather fond of one particular human, now asleep in the room on the other side of the window glass. For the past two nights, the cat's glowing eyes had kept watch over a slight girl who smelled of books and Sunlight soap and friendship.

A movement below caught the cat's attention. She paused in her toilette. Despite the great distance, she knew the object in motion was too large for a mouse, or even a rat. She fixed her golden gaze, watching, watching.

It was another human. But not a full-grown one. In all likelihood, it was harmless, but she couldn't tell for certain from her verticality. The cat stretched all along her spine, ending the undulation with a sharp flick of her tail. Soundlessly, she bounded from this railing to that fire escape to that peaked gable until she was four-footed on the street. She slunk from shadow to shadow until she was nearly upon the young human, who was apparently unaware of her presence. She studied him studying the hotel for an hour or more and then, as the streets began to churn with deliverymen and ash can collectors and others whose work requires early morning beginnings, the young human sauntered off.

The cat followed. Not because she did not trust the human. On the contrary: In him she sensed a comrade. But that trust had yet to be fully earned, so when the young human stopped, mid-block, looking behind him, unable to shake the feeling that he was being followed by someone or something, the cat ducked behind a spittoon. Her elegant tail flicked twice. The effect was to put the boy in such a fog that he ran full force into a lamppost, causing him to see stars. He wisely kept his eyes front and forward for the remainder of his journey.

The cat pattered behind him all the way to his nest, where he was greeted by another human, this one worn frail and rickety by age. The younger human towered over the older one, but was deferential—almost tender—in his actions toward him.

She lurked, well out of sight of the two humans, in the shadows of that place redolent of horses, before finding a satisfactory hiding spot behind a bale of hay. With the exception of her girl, most humans were so tedious and unimaginative. It was no challenge to hide from this pair. Min's ears twitched at the clinking and clanking of their morning routines. The younger one whistled as he washed up the breakfast dishes. The older one used a kind voice and only that to lead two solid horses, their flesh quivering against the chill, outside. For their "morning constitutional," he said. After man and horses and boy left, it was quiet in the space. Completely quiet. The cat did not even hear any mice scrabbling in the hay. Too bad. She would have enjoyed a snack.

Content that it was safe to venture out, to venture back to the hotel, the cat rubbed her side against the corner of the hay bale and delicately padded into the open.

She stopped.

There, not two rabbit hops from her hiding spot, sat a saucer of fresh cream.

She picked up one perfect white paw and licked it, considering. Clearly, she'd misread this pair of humans. Perhaps they belonged to the same tribe as her own girl. Odd that they'd never let on that they'd been aware of her presence. Curious, indeed. But the first thing every cat learns in kittenhood is the danger of satisfying one's curiosity. This pair must have had their reasons for leaving her be. And for furnishing breakfast. Whatever those reasons, they mattered not a whisker to Min.

She nosed at the saucer. It *had* been ages since supper. And she was growing weary of a constant diet of mice and tiny fowl. She sniffed. The cream spoke of clover fields and wobbly-legged calves and a warm shaft of sunshine in a cool barn.

The cat hunkered down, closed her eyes, and lapped up the entire saucer of the creamy liquid, purring all the while.

CHAPTER FIFTEEN

A Small Cog

Audie finished the fancy rolls and jam that Beatrice, the French maid, had brought for their breakfast. "Those were delicious." She picked up a flaky morsel with the pad of her index finger and popped it in her mouth.

"It was—" Beatrice waggled her hand, indicating mediocrity. "Nothing like the croissants *chez soi*. At home." She wrinkled her pert Parisian nose. "Not like Papa's."

"Did he teach you how to make them?" From a closer inspection of her plate, it appeared that Audie had gotten every last crumb. As Beatrice would say, *Quel dommage.*

Another nose wrinkle. "I did not inherit Papa's cool hands. So of the necessity for croissants. But he said I was a *pâtissière*—I think you say pastry chef—par excellence. He permitted me to make the *petits fours* for all the village festivals." Now Beatrice's brow wrinkled.

"You didn't want to be a pastry chef?" Audie inquired. There was such a long pause before the maid answered that Audie wasn't sure Beatrice had understood the question.

"Ah, *ma chérie*. Sometimes we do not know what we truly want until it is far too late." Beatrice removed a hairbrush from the bureau top and motioned for Audie to face the mirror. "But now, we must fashion the *cheveux*—how do you say it?" She tugged gently on Audie's curls, asking for the English word.

"Hair." Audie provided the translation, grateful once again for the *Conversational French* book at her bedside.

"Air," repeated Beatrice with a nod. With a whisk, whisk, whisk of the brush, she parted Audie's unruly locks, smoothing the front on each side into gentle waves and combing the rest of her curls into a soft, flowing tail at the neck. Beatrice caught that in place with an enormous navy-blue satin ribbon, starched stiff as a baguette. "*Voilà!* Monsieur le Commodore will be so happiness."

Audie smiled. "Thank you, Beatrice. He will be quite happiness." Underneath Beatrice's crisp and proper uniform, Audie had discovered, beat a heart as true as Bimmy's. In fact, our heroine was convinced that Beatrice and Bimmy would be best chums, should they ever happen to meet. A highly unlikely state of affairs. *Quel dommage* again. Audie twirled in front of the mirror. "I look respectable enough to be presented to the Queen of England!" She jutted her nose in the air.

"Or the Maharajah of India!" Beatrice folded her hands into a prayer and bowed.

"The King of Siam!" Audie dipped one knee.

"The Archduke of Austria!" Beatrice curtsied.

"The President of the United States!" At this suggestion, the two collapsed in laughter, hysterical at the outrageousness of such a notion: orphan meeting president.

Their glee was abruptly disturbed by a sharp rap, which coincided with the door swinging open. Cypher inflated himself in the doorway, driver's cap tucked under his arm.

"The Commodore is waiting," he said. "If you are finished with your shenanigans in here." He wore his disapproval like a badge.

Beatrice swept up the hairbrush and hairpins. "Mademoiselle's toilette is complete." She nodded, all business, to Cypher. But there was a wink for Audie as she turned to put the hair things away in the drawer. "What is the plan for Mademoiselle today?"

Cypher scarcely acknowledged Beatrice. "When such information is key to your services, it will be shared."

Beatrice's porcelain face grew prettier as she blushed. "*Eh, bien.* I shall be here again after the supper?"

He held the door and motioned Audie through. "Yes. After supper."

Audie took offense for Beatrice at Cypher's condescending tone. Imagining herself to be a personage whose importance matched her new frock and boots and hairstyle, she threw back her shoulders and passed, swishing to and fro, in front of Cypher. "Thank you, my good man," she said in her most imperious manner.

Beatrice's faint giggle traipsed after them into the hall. The Commodore was exiting his own room; Audie caught a whiff of gardenia through the open door. Her observational skills were put to the test as she took in the bouquets at each end of the long hallway. Vases burst with wintery holly and pine arrangements. Nothing of the tropical about them at all. But there wasn't time to decipher this olfactory conundrum.

"Come along, Annie. We mustn't be late." The Commodore took Audie's arm, propelling her toward the elevator cage.

"Where are we going?" The gold coin in Audie's right boot shifted and she shook her foot surreptitiously to move it back to the toe so she could walk more comfortably. "Are we finally going on the"—she lowered her voice to a whisper, confident that Cypher was far enough ahead not to overhear—"mission?"

"Tut, tut!" The Commodore put his finger to his lips. The metal cage doors creaked open. "Mum's the word."

The elevator operator let Audie push the button for the lobby; upon their arrival, she and the Commodore waited in the vestibule while Cypher fetched the car. The Commodore exchanged another mumbly conversation with the bellman while Audie counted the black tiles on the entry floor.

"Here we go." The Commodore held the hotel door for Audie.

"Fifty-seven," she said.

"What?" The Commodore looked perplexed.

"Tiles," Audie answered.

"Remember what I said." The Commodore flashed a forced smile. "Silence."

Audie nodded and climbed into the car when Cypher pulled it up in front of the hotel. As she slid over to the far side, she thought she caught sight of a newly familiar face. She leaned forward, seeking left and right.

"I can still hear you!" The Commodore glowered at her over the front seat.

Using only her eyes, Audie took one last look. No sign of Juice. No sign of anyone she knew. She quietly pulled the lap robe over her legs. Would today be the day that her role in the mission would be revealed? That thought warranted only a moment or two of cogitation. It was a bit like watching a pot boil: No amount of eye-strain could increase the speed of the desired end result.

Their automobile eased around a dawdling enclosed observation car—25 MILES OF SIGHTSEEING. DAILY TOURS. 50 CENTS—narrowly missing a squadron of beskirted young ladies who were propelling their smart new Racycle bicycles down Pennsylvania Avenue.

Since they'd arrived in the city, except for her adventure with Juice, Audie'd had little time to explore. It would be such a shame to return to Miss Maisie's with no stories to tell the Girls about the nation's capital. She vowed to instantly begin to put to memory all the wonderful sights and sounds around her.

As if he read her mind, Cypher spoke. "Turn quick, and you can see the monument."

So stunned at this offer of enlightenment, Audie nearly missed the glimpse of the Washington Monument behind them.

"Oh, thank you," she said. "It's much more impressive in person than on that postcard." Audie hugged herself. Wouldn't Bimmy love to see it. Rather, wouldn't Bimmy love to climb to the very tip-top, as high up—or higher!—than her high-wire parents? When her neck would turn no farther, Audie faced forward, in time for the Capitol to fill her view. The auto jogged around the Capitol grounds, and past the Botanic Garden—the triplets would so love to stroll there, perhaps among the flowers that were their own namesakes. She would endeavor to bring them in the springtime; on this December day, the gardens bore the look of an old tomcat worse for the wear after a few too many late-night alley fights.

A few more lefts and rights and lefts again, and the car turned down a street lined with small businesses. In front of one brownstone building, Cypher eased the auto up to a curb. "Shall I wait, sir?"

The Commodore was already extruding himself onto the sidewalk. "Return for us in an hour or so," he said. He got himself erect, smoothing overcoat, hat, hair, and moustache. "Come along, Annie."

Audie slid obediently out of the backseat and began to close the door behind her. "There's a food stall by Union Station," she told Cypher, thinking to repay his tour guidance with a bit of her own. "Lulu's. Ask for the special with a cup of joe. It's delicious!"

To her complete surprise, Cypher gave a nod. "I would enjoy a cup of coffee," he said.

She followed the Commodore up the steps of the trim brick row house endowed with the fanciful name of Rainbow's End, pausing at the glossy black door. Next to the entry, a directory proclaimed the businesses contained within. Audie doubted that she and the Commodore had come to pay a call on JOHN ALBEE, AUTHOR, or DOT DODGE, MANICURIST. That left MRS. ISABELLA WOODARD, LADIES EXCHANGE, SECOND FLOOR.

The Commodore puffed his way up the narrow stairwell, mopping his brow upon reaching the summit. The quiet within the building was no doubt explained by the fact that it was the lunch hour. The inhabitants had likely made their way to one of the nearby cafés. Audie's stomach gave a tentative little grumble itself at the thought of lunch. Croissants, though scrumptious, were not a sufficient breakfast for a growing girl.

The Commodore bypassed a closed office door whose neatly painted letters announced that said office belonged to the Mrs. Isabella Woodard listed on the directory below. A few steps down the hall, he gave a gentle rap on a similar door, though unmarked.

A tall woman answered, opening the door a narrow wedge. Her face put Audie in mind of a bird: her nose beaky, her eyes small and shiny. "Is this the girl?" The woman's accent was English.

Audie felt a thrill at the question. Perhaps the pot had finally boiled! Perhaps she would now learn her part in the Commodore's plan!

The Commodore nodded and the woman opened the door wider so they could step inside. For the second time that day, Audie caught a whiff of gardenia. The woman pointed to two chairs; both Audie and the Commodore sat.

"I suppose you know why you are here?" The bird woman squawked the question.

Audie glanced at the Commodore. She didn't want to answer incorrectly.

"I thought it best to keep her in the dark." The Commodore shifted on his chair.

After a brief pause, the woman nodded. "Yes, of course. The less she knows—" She let the thought hang in the air, unfinished.

Audie's imagination couldn't help but finish. The less she knows, the safer she is? Is that what was implied? Audie swiped damp palms on her new wool coat, inhaling deeply to steady her nerves.

"We have an exceedingly important job to do. Tomorrow. At the White House." The woman stared down her beak at Audie, her hot gaze warming Audie right through to her backbone.

The White House! That silly game she'd played with Beatrice hadn't been too far off the mark. The White House. What would the Wayward Girls say to that? Audie sat a little taller, shoulders back, pride puffing out her chest. Think of it! An orphan coming to the aid of the President of the United States.

"It's an honor." Audie couldn't help but wonder what sort of assistance the President might require of her. Though there could not be another man in America with more on his mind than poor Mr. Taft, it would hardly do for Audie to offer him bedtime songs such as those she had sung to soothe the triplets. She struggled to imagine what other help the nation's leader could demand of an orphan. Nothing came to mind. But nevertheless. The President needed her. And she was not about to let him down. By the time her thoughts cycled through all the possibilities, she was so full of patriotic fervor and passion she nearly saluted Madame Beaknose. "I'll do whatever you need."

The woman nodded curtly. "We haven't much time. Listen closely."

CHAPTER SIXTEEN

There Is No Accounting for Taste

Audie sat up in bed, tugging the coverlet to her chin, straining to listen. Once assured that Beatrice was breathing the gentle respirations of the sleeper, Audie peeled back the bedclothes and slid her feet to the floor. A shadow with a swaying tail had appeared outside the window nearly an hour before, but she hadn't dared take action, not with Beatrice bustling about.

"Perhaps you will get to meet Monsieur le President after all!" Beatrice had exclaimed, brushing Audie's hair into one-inch sections and wrapping each section around a strip of flannel, before tying the ends of each strip into a loose knot. By the time Beatrice was finished, Audie felt as if Miss Maisie's quilt scrap bag had burst open upon her head.

"Ooh la la." Beatrice had spun Audie around and kissed her on both cheeks. Audie had determined that this was something the French did when they greeted one another or when they parted or when they were excited or for nearly any occasion in between. "To meet such largeness!"

Audie had turned away, quickly. She was certain Beatrice was not referring to the nation's twenty-seventh president's girth—which *was* astounding, that could not be denied—but his *political* stature. The maid's misunderstandings of the English language could be so humorous at times.

"I doubt I'll get to meet the President," Audie had replied. "But if I do, I'll look more than presentable, thanks to you."

Beatrice had insisted on an early bedtime so Audie would be ready for her big day. Thankfully, Audie had been able to slip her daily postcard to the elevator operator, who promised to get it into the seven-thirty post. What with the beauty salon treatment and early donning of nightgowns, Audie would have had no opportunity to mail the card otherwise. Once she'd gotten Audie settled, Beatrice had had no trouble falling asleep herself. But then she did not know what Audie was going to be doing at the White House. Not that Audie could tell her—she'd been sworn to secrecy by Madame Beaknose.

Now assured that Beatrice was back home in Saint Cado, at least in her dreams, Audie slowly cracked open the hotel room window to allow entrance to her oldest and dearest friend.

"Hmm," Audie mused, when it became apparent that she would need to nudge the window open a bit wider than usual. "It looks like you've gained some weight, Min. City life must agree with you."

Such a tactless comment about her weight caused Min to pause on the windowsill, half in and half out of the room. But she pressed on, deciding to forgive Audie for her insensitive observation. After all, the young have much to learn about what one does and does not say to others. Min had caught a glimpse of herself that morning in the window of the Betsy Ross Candy Shop across the street from the hotel and thought herself looking the epitome of feline felicity. She found the rounded purse that swayed between her four paws to be quite comely indeed. It made her look every bit a cat of the world.

Min bounded onto the bed, kneading at the coverlet to show Audie that there were no hard feelings about her thoughtless remark. Audie climbed back under the sheets, scratching that delicious spot behind Min's left ear.

"Bees and bonnets, Min, you'd think I'd have been brought all this way for something really important, wouldn't you? I mean, it must have cost the Commodore a fortune to feed me and buy me all these nice new clothes. And for what?" Her head drooped to rest on top of Min's. "You'll never guess." She could hardly bring herself to say the words. Not even to her dearest friend. It was only Min's purr that gave her confidence to confess.

"I know it's important to keep the President happy, especially with all the hard work he has to do. I mean, can you imagine running this country? Keeping peace between the Democrats and Republicans? Between the farmers and the businessmen? Between the oilmen and the conservationists?" Audie's head began to ache a bit in sympathy for Mr. Taft. "And, with my own unseemly fondness for gingersnaps, I certainly know what it's like to suffer from food cravings. But honestly, Min." She could not bring herself to meet that pair of golden eyes. "Soup?"

Audie pushed herself away from her feline friend, slumping backward against the headboard. "I've been brought all the way from Miss Maisie's to help make the President's favorite soup. Which can only be prepared by a real English cook. And this particular real English cook can only work if she has an orphan for an assistant." Audie hung her head. "And not any soup, Min. Terrapin Soup." She made a face. "Turtle soup."

Min could tell that her friend was distraught. She corkscrewed herself into a ball next to Audie's left hip and remained there, radiating warmth and comfort, until Audie fell asleep. Audie squirmed in her dreams, dodging turtles paddling their flippers in murky green ponds, all the while wearing a copper kettle on her head and cooking mitts on her feet. Finally, the dreaming and squirming stopped and she began to engage in the soft, deep breaths of the young and innocent.

Satisfied that Audie was soundly asleep at last, Min slipped away, out the window, onto the ledge. Her every cat fiber tingled with concern. A mere *kitten* could put two and two together and figure out that Audie had not been brought all the way from Swayzee, Indiana, to Washington, D.C., to lend assistance in preparing a batch of turtle soup, no matter who was set to consume it. There was more to this kettle of fish than met the eye.

The cat bounded its way to the street below. It was time to enlist some assistance.

CHAPTER SEVENTEEN

An Unsettling Dream

Bimmy's arms flailed as she batted at something furry crawling over her face. She bolted up in bed, clutching at the bedcovers.

Her movements awakened the one triplet on her left and the two on her right.

"Something's wrong!" declared Lilac.

"Did my snoring wake you?" asked Lavender.

Violet took one look at Bimmy and hopped out of her own cot. "I'll make you some hot milk," she said.

"No, no. I'm fine. I'll be fine." Bimmy was comforted by the faces of her friends, made paler in the moonlight. Yet, she shivered as the last of the fleeting images of her nightmare evaporated.

Lilac and Lavender tugged the coverlet they shared to Bimmy's bed and tucked it around her shoulders. Her trembling eased.

"Was it a bad dream?" Lilac asked tenderly.

"It might help to talk it out," suggested Lavender.

Violet said nothing, but gently rubbed Bimmy's back.

After a few minutes, Bimmy sighed deeply. She had carried the burden of this nightmare all alone these past two nights. She could not bear it by herself any longer. "It was so dark," she began. "There was a room. A messy room full of castoffs—broken tools and kitchen utensils."

"Was that what frightened you?" asked Lilac.

"The room?" Bimmy shook her head. "No."

"But something did," prompted Lavender.

Bimmy nodded. "Everything was blurry, confusing. Remember that time we had a twirling contest?"

The triplets nodded.

"And that was scary?" Violet asked.

"No." Bimmy swallowed hard. "There was a bird-faced woman and a knife and something bad was going to happen. But there was no way out. The door was locked. Locked tight."

"And you were trapped," surmised Violet.

"That's the worst part." Bimmy covered her face with her hands, lowering her shaky voice. "It wasn't me in that horrible place. In that horrible situation." She shuddered, then grabbed Violet's hands. Lilac and Lavender gathered as close as they could to the other two girls.

"Not you?" Violet pressed.

Bimmy clamped her lips together. She stared into the dark for several full and wretched seconds. She dreaded speaking the words but she must. "It was Audie."

"Audie!" Lilac and Lavender gasped.

The girls trembled together in the darkened room. After a time, Violet bent to place a kiss on Bimmy's furrowed brow. "But you woke up before the dream was over, isn't that right?"

Bimmy nodded.

"Then let us recall what Audie has always told us." Violet summoned every ounce of bravery within her to comfort her sisters and her friend.

Together, the girls recited in a whisper so as not to waken the other Waywards asleep nearby: "Things will turn out splendid in the end. And if it's not splendid, it's not the end."

Bolstered by these words, the triplets crowded into Bimmy's bed where they cuddled in their joint and utter confidence in their absent friend and her abilities.

Bimmy, the dear thing, could not rest. The nightmare's bleak vision had shaken her to the core. She wanted to believe that things were going to turn out all right. But didn't Reverend Woolnough advise to "pray but swing the hammer"? Audie needed help. Bimmy was convinced of that. How on earth could she help her dearest chum when they were so many miles apart?

Bimmy tossed and turned like a seashell atumble in the tide. She was about to give up, give in to utter despair, when it came to her. There was a way she could lend assistance to Audie, despite the great distance between them.

Her heart grew light along with the morning sky. Bimmy had friends all over the country. Circus friends. And it stood to reason that some of those friends had to be performing in Washington, D.C.

Now all she had to do was figure out which friends those might be. Then she would send out the SOS.

CHAPTER EIGHTEEN

Ten O'Clock Sharp at the White House

The Commodore was fuming, though it did not interfere with his breakfast. Hardly anything, let alone a tardy chauffeur, interfered with his meals. "Where is that infuriating man?" He attacked the T-bone steak on his plate, a breakfast choice inspired upon learning that the President generally began his day in this same manner.

Audie did not know the answer to the Commodore's question. She had her own suspicions about Cypher, however; none of them good. She had no idea why he might want to gum up the mission, but she would not put it past him. If only the Commodore had taken her concerns about Cypher seriously. But he dismissed her every point. "Simply because the man makes a few telephone calls hardly makes him a criminal," the Commodore had told her. And he'd laughed aloud about Cypher's plump thumbs.

So rather than push the point now, with the Commodore so clearly in a dither, Audie wisely remained seated on the chair across the room, ankles crossed in precisely the manner prescribed in *Mrs. Paul's Manners for the Modern Girl*. It wasn't so much that Audie was keen on etiquette; rather, this pose gave her ample opportunity to admire her new boots. She wiggled her toes, reassuring herself that the gold coins were secure.

"You are to report to the kitchen at ten on the dot. If he makes you late . . ." The Commodore hinted at the consequences of such an action with a sharp slice of his knife through the air, flinging a blob of quince jelly onto his pristine white vest.

Audie suspected she should point out this flaw, but the Commodore was in such a state that she hesitated. It might be the one thing to send him completely over the edge. Yet, how would she feel if she went out in public with food on her new dress and no one told her? Audie uncrossed her ankles and stepped daintily over to the tea tray, removing her napkin and handing it to the Commodore.

"What?" He glanced down. "Oh, just my luck. Everything's all sixes and sevens." The Commodore dabbed impatiently at the spot. "Better?"

Audie leaned forward. "Almost." Relying on yet another tip from Mrs. Paul's handbook, she took the napkin from him, dipped it in the water glass, and finished the job.

The Commodore inspected her efforts, nodding with approval. He looked at her as if he'd only then realized she was in the room. "Why aren't you eating?" He took in her barely touched breakfast. "I can't have you fainting from hunger again today."

"I had some toast." Audie pushed at the crust on her plate. Her stomach *was* aflutter. Her task might seem small and insignificant, but it was still being asked of her by the President. Well, not directly of course, but one needn't put too fine a point on such things. She had traveled all these miles and this was the day she was to fulfill her destiny. She stood a bit taller at the thought.

The Commodore was shoveling in the last bite of steak when the buzzer sounded at the door. He waved to Audie to answer.

"The car is ready, sir." Cypher stood there, hat tucked under his left arm. Audie noticed a sheen of perspiration on his forehead and above his lip. Nerves at being late? Or something else? "I have already gathered Mrs. Finch."

The Commodore nodded, chewing vigorously as he wiped his hands on the linen napkin. He rose, shrugged into his jacket, and grabbed a last slurp of coffee. "Off we go, then."

Audie slipped into her own coat, buttoning it up to the neck, and then patted at the rosette Beatrice had pinned in her hair. She thought it added a festive touch.

"Very good, sir." Cypher stood aside to allow the Commodore, and then Audie, rucksack in hand, to pass. The Commodore had told her to take along her spare dress. "In case you get a spot on that one while you're cooking," he said. Beatrice had helped Audie fold the dress neatly into the rucksack. Audie'd thrown in her Reliable flashlight for good measure.

As Cypher had stated, Mrs. Finch was already in the automobile. The Commodore seated himself up front and Audie slid in back. She caught a whiff of something fragrant. Tropical. Could it be gardenias?

She glanced over at Mrs. Finch—Audie had to remind herself not to call her Madame Beaknose! She was knitting something— a blanket? a muffler? a sweater?—in the most hideous shade of yellow. The color put Audie to mind of some of the diapers she had changed when the triplets were infants.

She thought to ask if Mrs. Finch was knitting the unidentifiable item for someone special but hesitated. She definitely belonged to the seen-not-heard school of thought regarding children.

"I see you admiring my work." Mrs. Finch paused in her click-click-clicking to loosen more yarn from the ball in the bag at her feet. "Idle hands are the devil's playthings," she added.

"Yes, ma'am." Audie nodded, swinging her legs.

Mrs. Finch squinted. She raised an eyebrow.

Audie stilled her legs. "Is that a—?"

"Baby blanket, yes." Mrs. Finch held up her handiwork. "For my nephew."

"He'll be honored at such a gift." Audie watched Mrs. Finch's right hand slip the right needle into the loop of yarn on the left needle and then scoop that loop onto the right needle, all the while holding the yarn at the back of the stitch with her left forefinger. "That looks tricky," she added.

"Not at all." Mrs. Finch sniffed. "I learned when I was younger than you."

"Really?" Audie gave her a look of admiration. "Was that in England, where you grew up?"

"Yes." Mrs. Finch started another row. "In Upper Puddlebury by the Sea. My sainted granny taught me. She was a jolly old bird, was Granny Finch."

Audie smiled at the little joke though Mrs. Finch didn't seem aware she'd made one. "I read a book on knitting," Audie said. "But I haven't tried it myself yet. Maybe you could give me a lesson today." It would be such fun to whip up hats for the triplets, or a muffler for Bimmy. Maybe pot holders for Cook and face cloths for Miss Maisie and the rest. She would've thought that, being from Upper Puddlebury by the Sea, Mrs. Finch would knit in the English style, rather than the Continental. She recognized the technique from the few tomes in the Punishment Room that had belonged to Mrs. Witherton: *Knitting for the Refined Young Lady* and *The Joys of Purling*. Perhaps Granny Finch was not originally from the United Kingdom, but from Germany, where such an approach to knitting was more generally employed. "If there's time, that is."

Mrs. Finch scoffed. "Time! There won't be any time for knitting once we don our aprons, girl." She pointed a needle right at Audie's heart. "You're here to help cook and don't you forget it."

Audie scootched across the seat toward the door. Away from Mrs. Finch and her pointy needle. "No, ma'am. I won't."

The rest of the ride was quiet, except for Mrs. Finch's click-click-clicking. Audie got a little pinch in her chest with each and every click. Soon enough, they were rolling up to the service entrance. Two bored guards glanced at the car. It was astonishing, really, that the President was protected in such an informal and flimsy manner. But that is absolutely the case. One of the guards held up his hand, indicating Cypher to stop.

"Yes, officer?" Cypher's voice was syrupy.

"Business?"

Mrs. Finch leaned forward in her seat. "You'll get the business, if you don't let us through. I'm the English cook." Then she sat back, case closed.

The younger of the two men looked bewildered. But the older one waved them through. As they rolled beyond the wrought-iron gates, Audie could hear the younger one say, "Soup? She's here to make soup?"

Mrs. Finch rolled up her knitting project and stuffed it in her bag. "Pull up over there," she ordered Cypher, with a tap on his right shoulder. "That looks like the kitchen entrance."

He did as commanded.

The Commodore hoisted himself out of the auto practically before it came to a stop. He opened the door for the backseat passengers, giving the appearance of someone in a hurry. "Well, Annie. Mind your p's and q's."

"Yes, sir." Audie shivered in the chill morning air as she glanced around the courtyard. This clearly wasn't the fanciest part of the White House—it was a service entrance after all. But to think she was standing on the drive that might have been tread upon by such great men of history like Abraham Lincoln and Theodore Roosevelt and now President Taft. Her feet fairly tingled in her boots at such a notion. And even in this tucked-away corner, the grandeur of the nation's First Home was evident. The entire of Miss Maisie's School would fit in this one quadrangle!

Mrs. Finch took the Commodore's proffered hand and exited the car, as well. She gathered her bags. "Close your mouth, girl, and come along." The cook started for the great arched doorway directly in front of them. Audie knew she should follow but her feet would not move. Through those doors and she—Audacity Jones!— would be inside the White House. Inside the home of the President of the United States! Walking floors across which had stepped dukes and prime ministers and kings and queens. The thought made her shiver all over again.

The rumble of an automobile engine startled Audie out of her reverie. The Commodore and Cypher were preparing to depart. Mrs. Finch was out of sight. Probably already in the kitchen, wondering where Audie was.

Audie shook herself out of her woolgathering and broke into a run to catch up. And crashed right into a boy on a bicycle.

CHAPTER NINETEEN

Anything but the Punishment Room

The foursome huddled in their hidey-hole under the stairs, letting Bimmy's words filter over them like dust motes.

Bimmy finally broke the silence with a giant exhaled breath. "I wouldn't ask this of you unless it was important."

"Do you think it's really, *really* important?" asked Violet.

"As in imperative?" added Lilac.

"Maybe you misunderstood what she said." Lavender blinked back a tear. "How could the Punishment Room hold any answers?"

"Now, girls." Bimmy squared her shoulders. Her caramel-drop eyes bored into three identical pairs of pale blue ones. "Think of everything Audie has done for us." At this declarative, she allowed for a period of quiet, so that each girl could reflect on what they had been given in friendship without ever a thought of anything in return.

The triplets had been no bigger than paper dolls when their befrazzled parents left them in Miss Maisie's care. No one in the house had had a moment's sleep until Audie stepped forward and discovered that, though they *were* identical, the triplets were also three unique little beings. Violet needed a lovey to soothe her to sleep. So Audie sacrificed Percy to the cause, tucking the much-loved stuffed giraffe in the babe's arms. Lilac liked being toasty warm, a problem Audie solved by giving up her own baby blanket, hand crocheted in exquisite pink stitches by her mother. Audie swaddled Lilac up so tight that she took on the appearance of a little baby frankfurter snuggled in a pink wool bun. And, as it turned out, Baby Lavender required music to fall asleep. She was especially fond of "The Old Gray Mare." So Audie sang and sang and sang until the smallest of the triplets finally gave up her battle against slumber and cuddled with her sisters in their specially rigged-up crib for three.

While the triplets' memories cast back to *their* first days at Miss Maisie's, Bimmy reflected upon her own arrival. Her folks were circus people, best known for a rather astonishing high-wire act involving a wheelbarrow, a goldfish bowl, and a tuba. After years of performing in fifth-rate circuses, their big break finally arrived: the chance to headline in the Sircus Swisse. All they had to do was accept the circus master's three hard-fast rules: No dog acts, No bearded ladies (as a young man, his heart had been broken by Henriette the Hairy), and No children. Thus, four years previous, Bimmy had become Wayward Girl number 15, only six and ready to take a poke at the world before it could poke at her. Hers was the only dark face in the Swayzee sea of white. Bimmy had been standing in Miss Maisie's parlor, planning her escape not ten minutes after her arrival, when Audie caught sight of her signing the School roster.

"Look, Miss Maisie!" Audie had pointed at Bimmy, whose hands were already clenching into fists. "She's our first lefty!" And that was it. The end of Bimmy being assaulted by cruel names wherever she went. Labels that made bile rise up in her throat to recall. No. Here, at Miss Maisie's, in Swayzee, Indiana, she'd been dubbed Lefty. Or Southpaw. And her favorite, also bestowed by Audie: Best Chum. Not one of *these* nicknames did Bimmy mind wearing.

Bimmy shook away those remembrances, along with an unexpected tear. "We each owe Audie so much. How can we deny her aid in her hour of need?"

"But we don't all need to go." Lilac studied the tops of her worn boots. "Do we?"

Her sisters exchanged glances.

Bimmy nodded. "You're right. It's my idea." She inhaled deeply, summoning every ounce of courage in her small body. This could not be any more difficult than walking the high wire without a net, could it? And that was a task she could do blindfolded. And had done so on countless occasions. Bimmy put one foot forward. But the Punishment Room. She gulped.

"Oh, don't be ridiculous." Violet jumped up. "You're not going alone. We're in this together."

"We are?" whimpered Lavender.

"All for one, and one for all!" Violet stuck out her hand, and the others placed theirs on top in ascending order.

"It's now or never." Bimmy chewed on her bottom lip. "It's—"

"Bimmy, the more you talk, the harder it's going to be." Violet tugged her friend forward. "Let's get it over with."

With clasped hands, the four Wayward Girls wobbled down the dusty carpet, turning left at the third cabbage rose past the dining hall, marching to their doom in the Punishment Room.

CHAPTER TWENTY

Meeting Charlie's Father

Audie had never been kicked by a mule, but recent events had provided a reasonable approximation of that dubious pleasure. Her ears were ringing and her jaw throbbed—was that a loose tooth?—and she was acutely aware of every one of the two hundred and some odd bones in her body because each felt slightly out of joint, socket, or wherever else it belonged.

"Are you all right?" A freckled face swam into view.

She blinked.

"Are you unconscious?"

"Anything but." Audie tried to stand but her legs went on strike. The freckle-faced boy grabbed her before she crumpled again.

"Oh." The boy groaned. "Am I going to catch it from Father. Mother, too." He held on to Audie's arm while she got her feet under her. "Let me help you inside."

"No, no," Audie protested. "I'm fine."

The Commodore suddenly loomed over her. "That was a powerful collision. She might have suffered a concussion."

Mrs. Finch's face bobbed into view. The expression upon it sat at the opposite spectrum from concern.

The boy's freckles bleached. "A concussion!"

Before Audie could say anything more, Cypher swooped her up, and the boy led them—she, Cypher, Mrs. Finch, and the Commodore—through the arched doorway, away from the kitchen bustling with activity, into an office area. "Wait here," he said before running off.

"I'm fine," Audie insisted but the Commodore tut-tutted her.

"Can't be too careful, my dear," he said.

Cypher didn't say a word but from somewhere he brought Audie a glass of water. She took a grateful sip.

A short time later, the freckle-faced boy barreled back into the room. "They're coming," he announced. A few steps behind him appeared a dapper-looking bald man wearing a concerned expression on his face and carrying a black doctor's bag; two shakes of a lamb's tail later, an extraordinarily stout man arrived, with kind blue eyes, a proud Roman nose, and a salt-and-pepper moustache that put Audie to mind of walrus whiskers.

"What's all this?" the portly man asked. "Charlie says he's run you over."

"I'm fine," Audie repeated for what seemed like the tenth time. "Really I am."

The portly man patted his forehead with a bright white handkerchief. Cypher found him a chair and he sat, breathing hard. "We'll let Dr. Barker here make that decision, shall we?"

Dr. Barker felt Audie's arms and legs and listened to her lungs. He had her turn her head to the right and then to the left.

"See—still firmly affixed to my neck," she said. "Though I do seem to have lost my brand-new hat somewhere."

"Here it is." The boy had gone back for it and was brushing it off. "Is it supposed to look like that?" he asked.

Audie took it from him. The tip of the feather was broken clean off. Well, she hadn't been fond of that feather anyway. Too fussy. She removed it from the hatband and replaced the *chapeau* on top of her head. "It suits me better now."

"You're a pip." The boy grinned. He had a nice smile. A nice face.

"Actually, I'm a cook's helper." Audie glanced at Mrs. Finch, whose face looked practically vulture-like, and took another sip of water. She smoothed out her skirt. "And I'm perfectly fine. Mrs. Finch and I really need to get to work. The President will want his soup."

The adults in the room froze into a perplexing tableau. From their actions, Audie surmised that she'd said something wrong. But she hadn't one clue as to what that was. Then the portly gentleman threw back his head and roared.

"The President *will* want his soup, that he will." He dabbed at his eyes, he was laughing so hard. "It's a bit of a nuisance, I admit. But when you work as hard as I do, it doesn't seem unreasonable to dine on one's favorites at the end of the day."

The breath caught in Audie's throat. "Y-y-y-ou're—?"

The portly man stood, stepped closer, and held out his hand. "William Taft, at your service."

Audie glanced over at the freckle-faced boy. He grinned again. She slowly stretched out her right hand. Her fingers disappeared into the President's, hers David's to his Goliath's. They shook. "Audacity Jones," she squeaked out.

"Pleased to meet you, young lady." The President released his grip, then patted her head. "Are you certain you're not injured?"

Yet one more time, Audie assured those gathered that she was fine.

"All right, then. I have some work to do. And Charlie has a guest to entertain. One he seems to have forgotten all about." The President fixed his kind blue eyes on his son in a disapproving manner.

Audie recalled the newspaper mention of Dorothy Taft, paying a holiday visit to her aunt and uncle. From the sound of things, her cousin Charlie was being a neglectful host.

The grin vanished from Charlie's face. His head drooped. Even the lock of hair curled across his forehead seemed to droop. "Yes, Father."

* * *

Mrs. Finch was as hot as the stove by the time they got down to the kitchen. She was most displeased by the delay. "If I were ever to have children," she said, "I would only have girls. Boys are such ruffians."

"Well, this has been a peach of an adventure thus far, Annie, wouldn't you say?" Hat in hand, the Commodore beamed as if he had been personally responsible for arranging for Audie to meet the President.

Mrs. Finch slammed a cupboard door shut, bestowing a look upon the Commodore that was difficult to decipher. Audie could not determine if she was displeased at his comment or if her stomach had gone peptic over the recent obstacle to completing the soup on time. Mrs. Finch then slammed a drawer for good measure. "It's not proper for the likes of her to meet the President, if you get my drift," she snapped at the Commodore.

Audie quickly grabbed an apron and tied it around her waist, ready to work.

"No harm done, El—I mean, Mrs. Finch." The Commodore executed a hasty two-step around a work island. "I'm sure you're eager to get at it, eh? Soup's on, as they say!" He chuckled at his own tepid joke. "Shall we be back for the lot of you around four?"

"The lot of us?" Audie asked.

Mrs. Finch concentrated on the pots hanging from the rack above her head. "You mean, Annie and me, of course," she said.

"Of course," the Commodore blustered.

Having selected a pot to suit her needs, Mrs. Finch brought it down to the work surface with a clang.

The Commodore jumped, turning his hat uneasily in his hands.

Mrs. Finch clucked her tongue. "Be on your way. Some of us have got work to do."

"Mind Mrs. Finch, then, Annie." He plunked his hat upon his head, and swept out of the room, humming something that sounded a lot like "Wait Till the Sun Shines, Nellie."

Audie's left ear began to buzz. It wasn't that the Commodore's humming was unpleasant. He had a nice voice, a baritone; she'd told him on several occasions that he should consider joining the choir at the Methodist church.

She gently tapped at her left temple with the heel of her left hand. Maybe the crash with Charlie had caused some trouble in her ears. She tapped again, testing to see if that alleviated the buzzing.

"Girl, are you going to help me or not?" Mrs. Finch dumped a bowl of peeled onions on the worktable, rattling off a set of instructions.

Audie obeyed the Commodore's words. She did exactly as she was told. She pinned her hair bonnet—over the rosette—like that. Lined up the measuring tools thus. Gathered up the ingredients there. She followed Mrs. Finch's orders to the letter. To the very letter.

Mrs. Finch held out an enormous kitchen knife. Audie reached for it and began to chop. One of the regular kitchen staff was assembling a congealed salad at the other end of the long worktable. The young man smiled at Audie. "Ain't seen you before," he observed.

"It's my first time," said Audie.

"Ain't this kitchen somethin'?" He pointed upward with his index finger. "President Roosevelt put in this newfangled electric lighting system. Best light I've ever worked in." He gave his head a shake. "Though the buzzing can drive a fella mad sometimes."

Before Audie could say anything more, Mrs. Finch cut in. "She's here to help me," she said. "Not chatter." The look she shot the kitchen boy put an end to any further conversation.

Pondering the boy's words as she chopped a mound of onions, Audie soon convinced herself that the buzzing she'd heard when the Commodore departed had to be due to President Roosevelt's electric lighting.

It was the only explanation that made sense.

CHAPTER TWENTY-ONE

Inside the Punishment Room

The fact that Bimmy was shorter than Audie had never been worth noting. Now her lack of height was a gift of Providence. Had she stood eye-to-eye with the cyclops, as did Audie, Bimmy might never have found the courage to turn the tarnished black doorknob and enter the Punishment Room. Already terrified, Bimmy would have turned to stone to realize the creature *she* was staring at was a chimera.

She reached for the door. "Ready, girls?"

Three heads nodded.

"As ready as we'll ever be," Violet said.

Bimmy's fingers encircled the fat knob. She took another deep breath.

"Hurry!" Violet poked her in the back. "Someone's coming!"

With a quick twist of her left wrist, Bimmy spun the knob around, releasing the latch, and put her shoulder into the heavy door. It opened wide enough for the four of them to slip through and she quietly pushed it closed again.

Lavender—the shortest of the triplets—peered through the keyhole. "Divinity!" she whispered. The foursome froze in their places until they heard the self-satisfied tap-tap-taps of Divinity's boot heels pass along the hall and down the stairs.

"That was close," whispered Lilac.

The fear of nearly being caught by Divinity had briefly supplanted the fear of being in the Punishment Room. All too soon, the full realization of their location once again descended upon Lilac. She shivered. She sniffled. She tried the door. It wasn't locked. They could escape. She drew a shaky breath of relief.

"Look at this!" Violet stepped away from her sisters into the center of the enormous room, engaging in a slow turn. "Books!" Floor to ceiling. Wall to window. Across the way, a fire was laid. In front of the fireplace sat a plump wing chair and a side table. "Is that Jarlsberg?" Violet wandered over and broke off a bit of the cheese. "And look, gingersnaps, too."

"Don't eat anything!" Lilac rushed to her sister's side. "Might be poisoned."

Violet shrugged. "Tastes fine." She finished chewing. Cocked her head to the left. To the right. "See. Nothing to worry—" Her hands flew to her throat. She began coughing and gagging. She dropped to her knees.

Her sisters flew to her. "Violet! Violet!" Tears streamed down Lavender's face. "Don't die!"

"I told you not to eat it," Lilac sobbed.

Violet stopped coughing. She grinned. "Gotcha."

"Oh, you!" Lavender grabbed her sister's arms, pulled her upright, and began shaking her. "That was horrible." They wobbled around like a pair of tops, caroming off a pedestal table and setting an expensive-looking vase atwirl. Bimmy raced over and caught it before it crashed to the ground.

"That was a horrible joke to play," said Lilac.

"I'm never speaking to you again," said Lavender.

Bimmy held her head. Sisters! "Please don't forget the reason we're in here. And we've got to snap it up or we're not going to be any good to Audie at all." Bimmy's brain felt a bit like that file cabinet there in the corner—stuffed so full of papers and folders that it was nearly bursting open. Instead of papers, however, her mind was full of notions.

First, she was trying to fathom why such a place—such a wondrous place!—would ever have been called a place of punishment. Look at that section there: *Daredevils of the 17th Century*. And that cluster of books: *Flying Machines*. And those: *Stories from the Orient*. Why, this was heaven on earth! There would be words with Audie, yes there would, about why she'd kept this astonishing room under her hat for so long. So unlike her to be selfish. But then again, Bimmy knew not to judge another without trying on her pinafore and boots. Being an orphan must have its secret sorrows and secret needs, of a nature that a Wayward Girl might find it hard to understand. All right, then, Bimmy decided. She would not hold a grudge against Audie about the Punishment Room. And she would hope that, in her own good time, Audie would explain her secret keeping.

"Bimmy?" Lilac tapped her on the arm, bringing her back to the task at hand. Which was to figure out how they might find a way to help Audie in this very room. Hadn't Audie said the Punishment Room held answers? But how? Where to begin? "The clock's struck two. Miss Maisie . . ."

Bimmy didn't wait for Lilac to finish the sentence. Miss Maisie would be up from her after-lunch nap soon. No time to dawdle! She made a quick plan and barked out orders to the triplets. "My parents had this big book. *Daley's Circus Almanac.* It was how they knew which circus was performing where."

Violet ran her fingers along the closest bookshelf. "And that book is in here?"

It was not in Bimmy's nature to be dishonest. But it was in her nature to be optimistic. "Yes," she said with great optimism. "Yes." It must be, mustn't it? From the looks of things, nearly every other book in the world resided in this room. "But I've no idea where."

The four friends scrambled around the room, searching high and low. With every tick of the big grandfather clock in the corner, the muscles in Bimmy's neck drew tighter and tighter. She would not admit to the triplets that her faith was dimming. Where was that doggoned book anyway? It had to be here. Just had to. But it wasn't with the other almanacs. Nor with the As. Nor with the Ds. They'd looked everywhere.

Nothing.

Violet nibbled on another bit of cheese. "Maybe we're looking in the wrong places."

"I would think that was perfectly obvious." Bimmy made a face. "Otherwise, we'd have found it by now." She cringed at her tone of voice, which was a perfect snide echo of Divinity's.

Lavender caught sight of herself in the big mirror behind the dictionary table. "My braid's come undone. Will you fix it, Bimmy?"

"Now?" What did a little mussy hair matter at a time like this?

"I can't work with my hair a mess." A tear threatened to spill out of Lavender's lower lid.

Bimmy gritted her teeth but motioned Lavender over. Audie would entertain this foolish request, that Bimmy knew. The little girl plunked down on a footstool to make it easier for Bimmy to minister to her braid.

"Tell me one more time what we're looking for?"

Bimmy nearly tugged Lavender's braid in frustration. How dare she ask after they'd been looking all this long while? She answered through clenched teeth. "We're looking for a book called *Daley's Circus Almanac*." Bimmy finished off the braid and retied Lavender's ribbon. She stepped back, fingers tugging at the locket her mother had given her the first time she'd performed *sans* net. That had been such a moment of triumph. But this moment—"I'm afraid it's not here." Bimmy's heart pinched to think of letting Audie down in her hour of need.

"It must be, don't you think? This library has every book imaginable." Lavender swung around on the footstool. She blinked her blue eyes. "Maybe we should look under C for circus," she said.

Bimmy stared at Lavender. Then she snatched her off the footstool and twirled her around. "C for circus! Of course!" She set Lavender down and ran to the C section of Mr. Witherton's expansive library, and there, completely out of order and making no sense at all, she found exactly what she was looking for.

She snatched the book off the shelf and plopped it on the floor, running her finger from the top of each page to the bottom, flipping as fast as she could skim.

Lilac looked at the big clock over the mantel. "Better hurry, Bimmy."

"I am!" Bimmy's finger raced up and down the pages.

"Have you found anything yet?" Lavender asked.

"Let her concentrate," said Violet.

"But it's nearly two-thirty!" Lavender fretted.

Bimmy's heart was in her throat. Only a few pages remained in the almanac. She turned them, searching intently. Then her finger stopped. Circus Kardos. "Madame Volta," she exclaimed. "And Igor. It's perfect!" She looked up at her comrades. "Now all I need is for you three to create a diversion. Will you do it?" She snatched a piece of paper and pencil from Mr. Witherton's desk and copied down an address from the almanac.

"In for a penny, in for a pound," said Violet.

"Oh boy," said Lavender.

"You can say that again," said Lilac.

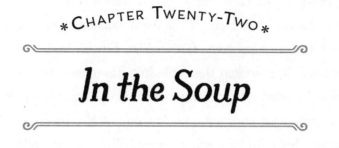

In the Soup

So far, the most exciting thing about being the soup maker's helper had been scrubbing the bottom of the copper soup kettle with baking soda and lemon juice.

"Elbow grease, girl." Mrs. Finch tackled a butcher block with a bristle brush and bleach water. "I should be able to see myself in that pot."

Audie applied the elbow grease of ten girls before satisfying Mrs. Finch. Then she filled the kettle with ten cups of water and was ready to add twelve whole cloves—"not ten or eleven, but twelve," ordered Mrs. Finch—when the jingling of harness bells was heard outside. Audie dropped in the twelfth clove and ran to the window.

A horse clip-clopped into the courtyard, pulling a wagon painted with a colorful logo for the Zastrow Brothers Fish Stall at the Center Market. "Whoa, there, Jem." The swarthy deliveryman hopped down from the driver's seat, tossing the reins over the back of the steady steed as he did so. Jem looked as if he had no intention of moving, ever again. Audie spied a small apple in an enamel-ware bowl on the table opposite and snatched it up. She weaved around the cook's helpers in the main kitchen, then scurried out through the open doorway, fast on Mrs. Finch's heels.

Jem's soft lips worked the apple into his mouth and he chewed contentedly while the deliveryman unlatched the wagon's doors. He wrangled an enormous bucket out of the back—it was big enough to hold Audie—and staggered through the arched doors, along the narrow main kitchen, and to Mrs. Finch's workstation.

"Where do you want 'em?" he asked.

In answer, Mrs. Finch pointed to a deep sink. The man upended the bucket, and out slid a dozen green turtles, mouths opening and closing, as if calling out to Audie, their fins cutting through the air as they had cut through the water in Audie's nightmare the night before.

Mr. Zastrow started to carry out the empty bucket.

"Oh, leave that, please." Mrs. Finch wiped her hands on her apron. "I'll use it for the shells."

The deliveryman nodded. "I'll pick it up tomorrow, then." He took the cup of coffee Mrs. Finch pressed on him before she turned to the sinkful of turtles. The first one was plucked out and plopped onto the chopping block. It turned its oval head toward Audie, its eyes meeting and holding hers.

Now, it wasn't that Audie was a vegetarian. She herself was fond of chicken and dumplings and had on more than one occasion assisted Cook in dispatching a hen in preparation for Sunday supper. It may well have been that Audie was still a bit out of sorts after having been run over by the bicycle. Or perhaps the buzzing in her left ear was having a greater impact than she realized. Or perhaps she should have eaten more for breakfast than one piece of dry toast. Whatever the reason, after locking gazes with that turtle, when Mrs. Finch picked up the cleaver and drew back her arm, it was more than Audie could bear.

CHAPTER TWENTY-THREE

Pirate's Pledge

Charlie glanced at the clock and stifled a yawn. Mother and Father had given him strict instructions not to abandon Dorothy again. They were up to their eyebrows in preparations for the big New Year's Day reception.

Actually, it was more like Mother was up to her eyebrows in preparations and Father was up to his eyebrows fretting about whether it was all too much for Mother. It would be her first official social event since the stroke.

"How about another round of charades after lunch?" Dorothy asked.

Charlie's eyes nearly spun 'round in his head. If there was anything more deadly dull than charades for two players, he couldn't think what it might be. "I've no more ideas of what to act out," he said.

"Well, then." Dorothy pouted. "It's your turn to think of something to do."

Charlie exhaled through flared nostrils. His turn! His turn! Every time he'd suggested something halfway diverting, she'd gone all floofy on him. "Oh, I can't do that. Oh, I can't do this." Gee willikers. Why did God make girls anyway? Total waste of time, as far as he could see. Well, maybe not that girl this morning. She was a pip. Dorothy could take lessons from *her*.

His cousin picked up her cup and sipped at the hot chocolate. "I'm having such a grand time." She sighed. "I wish I could stay longer."

Charlie managed to turn his groan into a cough. He reached for his water glass.

Dorothy eyed him over her cup. "You think I'm a huge bore, don't you?"

Though Charlie wanted to agree with her, good manners—and the thought of her reporting his reply to his parents—kept him from answering. "What about a game of Spite and Malice?" he countered.

"I hate playing cards," Dorothy answered. "I always lose."

Charlie sighed in utter defeat. "I guess it's charades, then." He could hardly believe he was saying those words. But maybe if he was extra-nice to Dorothy, Mother would let him have his bicycle back sooner.

"What about one of the games you play with your friends at school?" she asked.

Charlie could just see her going at cops and robbers. Or stickball. Or Pom Pom or Blindman's Bluff.

"You think I can't play at boys' games?" Dorothy sat up tall. "Try me." There was a glitter of determination in her eye that Charlie had not seen before.

"Well—" Charlie nearly suggested something, then stopped himself. "What if you get mussed up? Or skin your knee? You'll go crying to Mother and then I'll be in for it."

"I won't tattle." Her eyes shuttered into straight lines. "Pirate's pledge."

"Do you know what you're saying?" Charlie leaned forward in his chair. "There's no backing down from a pirate's pledge."

Dorothy tossed her curls back and grinned. From this angle, she carried the look of a pirate about her. Definitely the look of a pirate. "Oh yes. I know what I'm doing."

"Deal." Charlie spit in his palm. Held out his hand.

Dorothy spit, too. Met his hand. Shook. Hard. "So what's the game?"

This would be like taking candy from a baby. But Charlie felt remarkably free from guilt. "Hide-and-seek," he said.

"That's so easy." Dorothy sounded disappointed.

Charlie grinned wickedly. "Not the way I play it." He wondered how long it would take her, once she'd found her perfect hiding spot, to deduce that she was not being sought. That stubborn set to her jaw led him to believe it could be as long as half an hour or so. Maybe long enough to read another few chapters in *Five Children and It.*

"May the best man"—she arched an eyebrow—"or woman, win."

"One, two, three," Charlie began to count.

"You'll never find me!" Dorothy skipped from the room.

"That's the entire idea," he muttered under his breath.

CHAPTER TWENTY-FOUR

A Little Sleight of Hand

Bimmy did wish she'd had more time to devise a plan, but that was not to be. The telegram had to be sent right away and there was one method and one method only of getting into town and back: the bicycle that had been Miss Maisie's gift to the Waywards. Of course it had to be the day for Divinity's turn. It couldn't have been Katy or someone more amenable. Such is life.

"So all I need is a diversion," Bimmy repeated to the triplets.

"Like a sudden scream?" suggested Lilac.

Bimmy held back a sigh. "Well, in that vein of course, but something longer lasting. You have to keep Divinity occupied for at least an hour." Pedaling as fast as she could, to town and back, would take Bimmy a solid hour. It would be brutal but there wasn't much choice. Divinity was a pill but she was not simple; much more than an hour and she would guess that Bimmy was up to something.

"We'll think of the perfect diversion, Bimmy dear. Don't you worry." Violet patted their pal on the back. "Have you figured out the telegram?"

Bimmy recited the missive from memory: "Madame Volta and Igor stop Need a catcher pronto for my friend Audacity Jones Ardmore Hotel Washington DC stop Love Bimmy."

"Catcher?" Lavender's forehead wrinkled.

"They'll know what it means." Bimmy smiled. "Never you fear."

"So, sisters. Bimmy has *her* plan. What is ours?" Violet first looked at Lilac and then at Lavender. "A diversion that lasts at least one hour."

"Hmm." Lavender twirled a blonde curl around her finger. "What if we hide her buttonhook so she can't do up her boots?"

Violet patted her sister's hand. "That's the spirit. The thing is, what would keep her from borrowing someone else's buttonhook?"

Lavender looked downcast. "Oh, I didn't think of that."

"Lock her in her room?" suggested Lilac.

"She could climb out the window," Violet said.

"A sleeping draught in her milk?" Lavender threw in hopefully.

"Where would we get such a thing?" Violet shook her head. She put the kibosh on every one of her sisters' next dozen suggestions.

"I give up." Lavender plopped to the floor, her knees tucked under her chin. "I can't think of another thing. And now all of this scheming has made me starving."

"Go see if Cook can give you a sandwich," Lilac suggested absently.

"Cook." Violet stood a little taller. "Good old Cook." She began to hum. "That's it." She conferred with her sisters and, amidst much giggling and hand waving, they settled on their diversion.

It had been ages since the Waywards had held a taffy pull. And Divinity had not one sweet tooth but twenty-eight. There was nothing she could resist less than taffy. And there was nothing Cook could resist less than the smallest of the triplets batting her blue eyes, begging for a taffy pull.

As everyone knows, it takes at least one hour to pull taffy. At least.

The triplets offered to save Bimmy several pieces to enjoy upon completion of her mission. With lightning speed, she pedaled the bicycle into Swayzee, and placed her telegram order at the Western Union office. Within fifteen minutes came a reply. *Consider your friend caught stop Madame Volta.*

With a light heart, Bimmy cycled home, right on time to help Cook and her fellow Waywards snip the ropes of taffy into bite-sized bits and wrap them up in waxed paper, twisting the ends to keep them fresh.

"Delicious," Divinity mumbled with her mouth full.

"Yes," Bimmy agreed wholeheartedly. "This day has certainly been delicious."

CHAPTER TWENTY-FIVE

In the Dark

"There, there." A woman with a Canadian accent ran a cool cloth over Audie's forehead. "Ah, good. The pink's coming back to your cheeks."

Audie struggled to sit, trying to orient herself to her surroundings. Where was the kitchen? Mrs. Finch? Had she deserted her post twice in one day? What was the Commodore going to think of her?

"Like to have caused a goodly mess, if it hadn't been for Mr. Zastrow. He dropped his coffee and caught you the moment your head was about to connect with the floor." The woman reached behind her for a glass of water and brought it to Audie's lips. "Take a sip."

Audie did. "Where am I?"

"My office," the woman answered. "I'm Mrs. Jaffray. Head housekeeper. We're around the corner from the kitchen. When you're feeling up to it, I can escort you back."

"The turtles." Audie groaned, remembering. "They had faces!"

Mrs. Jaffray clucked her tongue, stroking Audie's forehead again. "That's over and done now. Best not to think on it much."

Audie blinked her eyelids furiously as if that action might sweep away the image of those poor turtles. "How can he eat such a thing?"

Mrs. Jaffray shrugged. "I imagine you eat all sorts of food without giving much thought to its origins, wouldn't you say?"

Audie had to admit that had been so in the past. But she could see herself changing her ways in the future. She took another sip of water. "I'm feeling much better. Mrs. Finch will be so cross."

"Not so cross." Mrs. Jaffray winked. "I poured her a lovely glass of sherry. You're sure you're up to getting back at it?"

Audie nodded.

Mrs. Jaffray escorted Audie to the kitchen, sniffing at the soup simmering away in the copper kettle, looking for all the world like any other stew. There was not a trace of turtle—shell, foot, or flipper—anywhere in the kitchen. Mrs. Finch had that much kindness in her, at least.

"I'll leave you to it, then," said Mrs. Jaffray. "The First Lady will be in a dither that I've been gone so long." In a symphony of rustling skirts, she hurried away.

Audie found a huge pile of carrots waiting to be peeled and chopped and she undertook that task with only the tiniest of glances from Mrs. Finch.

Finally, the woman rummaged in her pocket to pull out a tablet. "Here, chew on this." She handed it to Audie, who took it and, seeing no other option, put it in her mouth and began to chew. Her mouth brimmed with ginger and, right away, she felt put to rights.

"Thank you," Audie said, and sincerely.

"Ginger's the ticket for a squirrelly tummy." Mrs. Finch whacked a head of garlic into smithereens. Garlic did not affect Audie as did turtles.

Mrs. Finch reached for a bunch of parsley and began to chop chop chop away. "Might you run to the cooler? I will need another bunch of parsley. This one's far too small." She consulted a hand-drawn map thumbtacked to the wall next to the range. "It appears to be around the corner and down the hall."

Audie started in the direction Mrs. Finch indicated with her finger. For such a fancy house, the hall behind the kitchen was awfully dark. Not a window to be seen. The hall narrowed and split into two even narrower, even darker hallways that jigged this way and that. Old furniture hunched weary and sad in each nook and cranny. And many of the rooms in this damp and dreary space seemed to serve no useful purpose at all.

Finally, Audie opened a door and was lapped with a wave of cool air. She stepped into a room that smelled earthy and raw, like Cook's root cellar at Miss Maisie's. Audie scolded herself for not thinking ahead to bring her Reliable flashlight or at least a box of matches to light her way. She felt along the clammy walls, hands bumping over mason jars that she imagined were filled with peaches and green beans and mincemeat. She kept feeling, intent on finding the cool green sprigs of parsley Mrs. Finch required.

Her fingers moved from smooth glass to something soft and hairy. Something that moved.

The thing screamed.

And so did Audie.

CHAPTER TWENTY-SIX

An Innocent Pair of Tourists

Stanley, one of the Ardmore Hotel bellmen, hurried to assist the most recently arrived guests. The pair was laden with bags, all stenciled with CIRCUS KARDOS, but the young man—with hands as large as loaves of bread—fended off any help. Stanley tried not to stare, but the man carried three suitcases under one arm and four under the other and all with great ease. He had never seen such impressive biceps in his life. In contrast to the young man's massiveness, his traveling companion was a diminutive young woman in a stunning emerald velvet dress. Despite her petite appearance, she commanded attention as she made her way to the front desk.

"We have a reservation," she said, her clear English edged with a mere hint of her native Hungarian. "Madame Volta and Igor."

The front desk clerk smiled. "And what is Mr. Igor's surname?" he inquired, pen poised to complete the registration book.

"We would like that bellman to show us to our rooms." Madame

Volta pointed at Stanley, who by no small coincidence happened to be Elva Finch's brother. This was the same bellman with whom the Commodore had carried on those many whispered conversations.

"But I need Mr. Igor's full name for our register," the clerk protested.

Madame Volta leaned across the counter, peering intently into the clerk's pupils. "It is of no significance," she purred.

The clerk blankly batted his eyes. The pen dropped to the countertop and rolled onto the floor. He didn't pick it up. "It is of no significance," he repeated, his voice devoid of emotion. Then he rang for the bellman. "Show Madame Volta and Igor to their rooms."

As Stanley led the guests to the elevator, the clerk shook his head. How did his pen end up on the floor? It was his favorite Swan fountain pen, too. He picked it up, feeling pleasantly refreshed and renewed. He greeted the next guests with extra warmth and verve before efficiently signing them in.

The entire elevator ride to the sixth floor, and then down the hall, Igor retained a firm grip on all of the bags. Stanley surmised that there would be no tip coming from this duo. He could scarcely contain his irritation at this fact as he unlocked room 627. "There you are, miss."

The gorilla man carried the bags inside, and set them down before closing the drapes.

Madame Volta unclasped her crocodile-skin handbag. Stanley lingered. Perhaps there would be a tip after all.

"May I show you around the room?" he offered.

"I am interested in a different sort of information." Madame Volta removed a large bill from her bag.

The hairs prickled on the back of Stanley's neck. Elva had warned him not to shoot his mouth off. "I'll answer if I can, miss."

"Of course." She smiled and something loosened in Stanley's knees. He had never seen eyes that shade of blue before. They were almost violet, really. "There is a girl staying here, an Audacity Jones, is there not?"

"Oh, I'm not allowed to talk about the guests." Stanley stepped back. Those eyes. They weren't really violet, either. Maybe storm-cloud gray?

The young woman waved the bill. "We are old friends of hers."

"I can't—"

Madame Volta peered intently into his eyes. "Tell us about Audacity Jones," she purred. Stanley saw stars.

"Audacity Jones," he began, his voice as flat as the lobby's marble floor.

A few minutes later, Stanley boarded the elevator, on his way back to the bellmen's station. There was no large bill in his pocket. There was no memory of his conversation with Madame Volta, either. For some odd reason, he felt sweetly refreshed and rested. He even whistled merrily as he assisted a crotchety elderly couple with their numerous and weighty steamer trunks.

Up in room 627, Madame Volta and Igor discussed the information Stanley had unwittingly provided them. It was a goodly bit of knowledge indeed, but they weren't certain yet how they would use it to help Bimmy's friend, Audacity Jones.

CHAPTER TWENTY-SEVEN

Dorothy Plots Revenge

The dark room crackled with the sound of shattering glass and the smell of sugary syrup and cinnamon.

Someone let out a sharp cry of pain.

It wasn't a rat after all.

Nor was it parsley.

"Are you all right?" Audie stumbled backward, fumbling for a light switch. Perhaps this room had electric lights, as did the main kitchen.

"Yes." A pause and a sharp intake of breath between teeth. "No. No. I'm afraid I'm cut."

Desperately, Audie scrabbled at the wall and through sheer blind luck found the switch plate. She wrenched the knob on.

The light revealed a girl. A girl slightly older than Audie, whose hand was bleeding onto a delicate blue voile dress.

"Bees and bonnets. Let's get some help." Audie whipped off her apron and employed it in binding up the girl's wound. "This way." She led the girl to the kitchen, from whence Mrs. Finch summoned Mrs. Jaffray. Again.

Mrs. Jaffray turned white at the sight of the wounded young girl. "Miss Dorothy!"

Dorothy! Audie flinched. She should have instantly recognized her from the newspaper photograph. In her wildest dreams, Audie never could have imagined causing grievous injury to the President's niece. What a mess she was making of things.

Mrs. Jaffray led Dorothy to a chair and sat her right down. "Go fetch some water and soap and rags," she ordered Audie. Audie fetched as quickly as she could, hoping to make some small amends.

Mrs. Finch stepped away from the simmering soup long enough to inspect the wound and announce, "It will heal nice and clean."

"What on earth were you doing in the pantry?" Mrs. Jaffray asked.

Dorothy sighed. "Waiting to be found. But I've realized that was part of his evil plan."

"Evil plan?" Mrs. Jaffray froze in the middle of administering first aid.

"She's talking nonsense." Mrs. Finch grabbed the basin of pink water. "Go empty this and bring fresh," she ordered Audie.

"Charlie." The girl rubbed at the stain on her skirt with her free hand. "I should have known there was a catch when he suggested a game of hide-and-seek."

Audie set down the basin of fresh water, glimpsing tears in Dorothy's eyes. "The catch was that he had no plans to come seek," she guessed.

Dorothy nodded.

"See, I told you. Nonsense." Mrs. Finch looked oddly relieved. "All this fuss over a game."

"Oh, that's rotten." Audie reflected on her initial positive impression of Charlie. All because he had a nice, friendly face. Once again, she was reminded that a book could not be judged by its cover.

"Never you mind about Charlie." Mrs. Jaffray tended to Dorothy's cut. "You sit here for a bit. Calm down. Catch your breath." She glanced at the clock on the wall. "Mrs. Taft will likely have another stroke if I don't get back up there . . ."

"We'll keep an eye on her," Audie offered.

"And brew her a spot of tea," Mrs. Finch added, her voice chummy. "Right, Annie?"

"Nothing like a cuppa to cure all woes," Mrs. Jaffray said.

"Just the ticket," agreed Mrs. Finch. "You go on about your duties, Mrs. Jaffray. Miss Dorothy will soon be feeling put to rights."

"Why ever do these things happen with so much going on?" Mrs. Jaffray wondered. She took one last glance around the kitchen. "You're sure you can manage the soup *and* the girl?"

"Of course." Mrs. Finch bustled about, setting a kettle to boil. "I've got my own favorite tea, right there in my bag." She instructed Audie to slice up some cake while she took down a teapot and a cup.

Audie took note of the single cup. The morning had been trying; some tea would work wonders. But clearly she was not going to be offered any. She resumed her chopping and grinding.

"He thinks I'm a dreadful nuisance." Dorothy picked a corner off one of the slices of Sally Lunn cake that Audie had set out.

"Of course he doesn't," Audie said, despite her personal preference for truthfulness. It must be said that there are occasions when nothing but a tiny white lie will suffice. This appeared to be one such occasion.

"Maybe I should get even with him." Dorothy nibbled another bite of cake. "What if I didn't show up at supper? I could pretend I was still hiding. I would hate to worry Aunt Nellie so, but Charlie would catch heck, wouldn't he?"

Audie hesitated. Having been at the butt end of many of Divinity's mischiefs, she well knew the sweet temptation of revenge. How delicious was that plan to exact punishment on someone who had treated you cruelly. And there was the rub: The plan itself might be delicious, but the second one took the first step toward putting it into place, one was no better, no different, than the person who had been the initial cause of one's mistreatment. Audie long ago made the choice to follow the life advice she'd learned in one of Mr. Witherton's books: Keeping score only works in baseball. "The fact that you were injured might be painful enough for him," Audie said, blinking her eyes at the powerful fumes of the herbs she was crushing.

Dorothy held up her bandaged limb, studying it. "Of course, you're right." She let her hand drop. Gently. "Besides, no one would notice if I truly disappeared." The wistful look on her face pained Audie.

"I'll bet you're ready for that tea now." Mrs. Finch bustled around, filling the cup.

Dorothy glanced at Audie, then at her hand. "Yes," she said. "I suppose I am." She took the cup from Mrs. Finch, blew on it, taking a tentative sip. "It's awfully sweet."

"Drink up." Mrs. Finch hovered over her like an owl over a mouse. "You'll feel ever so much better in no time." Then she sniffed the air. "Oh, that soup is smelling lovely." She converged upon the copper kettle, taking up the tasting spoon to sample the simmering contents. "Fair, fair," she pronounced, smacking her lips energetically. "But it still needs that parsley." A jerk of her head was all the instruction she gave to Audie.

In all the excitement, Audie had forgotten her assigned task.

"I'll keep you company," Dorothy offered.

Before Audie could accept, Mrs. Finch held up her hand. "No, no, my dear. You are to rest. And finish your tea."

Audie started once again down the dark, narrow hall, tapping at her left ear. That scream Dorothy had let out earlier had set her eardrums to tingling. She shook her head to clear them.

To save herself yet another trip, Audie wisely appropriated two bunches of parsley. The sharp, fresh scent instantly took her back to the kitchen at Miss Maisie's. At the first hint of a Wayward sniffle, Cook would brew up a batch of chicken broth, fairly green with parsley. Cook insisted it was the next best thing to cure a cold. Her *preferred* remedy involved eating an entire raw onion, but that was a prescription few of the Girls could swallow.

In the cool dark of the pantry, Audie felt a pang of longing for Cook, for the School, and especially for her four best friends. Then she thought of how low Dorothy had seemed. How selfish to think of herself at this moment. In a flash, Audie had the most marvelous idea. Maybe Dorothy's spirits would be bolstered by having seventeen pen pals! That would surely make her feel wanted. Audie had a grand plan in place by the time she returned to the kitchen. But there was no sign of the President's niece.

"Where's Dorothy?" Audie asked.

Mrs. Finch was breathing hard and her bun was askew. "What? Oh, gone back upstairs."

Audie could not hide her disappointment. Dorothy's company had been a pleasant diversion. "Well, here's the parsley." How foolish to think someone of Dorothy's station would need the friendship of one Wayward Girl, let alone seventeen.

"Parsley?" Mrs. Finch stared at her blankly. "Oh. Yes. Wash it, chop it up, and add it to the soup." She pushed her bun back into place, before pouring out the leftover tea and scrubbing out the teapot. Audie felt a pang to see all that perfectly good tea go down the drain. She certainly would have enjoyed a cup herself. Resigned, she stepped over to the big sink, trying to block the image of the turtles scrabbling in it earlier.

She rinsed the two bunches of parsley, shaking off the excess water. One sprig went flying to the floor next to the turtle bucket and she bent to pick it up.

The lid was closed tight over a fragment of blue voile. Audie's ear buzzed as if an entire hive had taken up residence. She caught her breath. With trembling voice, she asked, "Where did you say Dorothy had gone?"

"I told you. Upstairs." Mrs. Finch was drying the teapot and turned to look at Audie. Our heroine had no experience in keeping expressions of horror from her face. Sadly, Mrs. Finch read what was there in an instant.

"My dear." Her voice dripped with insincere solicitude. "You look as if you've seen a ghost." She reached for a teacup that Audie had not observed earlier. "Here, do drink this. It will steady your nerves."

"No thank you." Audie stepped away from the turtle pot. "I'll be fine."

"I insist." Mrs. Finch reached for the very cleaver with which she had dispatched the turtles.

Audie felt she had no choice. She drank the tea. Dorothy was right: It was awfully sweet.

"Follow me." Mrs. Finch led the way to a darkened room. She opened the door and motioned Audie in.

"Please," Audie begged. "Do let's talk about this."

Mrs. Finch grabbed Audie's arm. "It was such a simple plan. All we had to do was go into the kitchen with one girl and leave with another. We had it all worked out. The posh set can't resist having the likes of us fuss over them." She struck a pose. "Oh, my helper would so love to meet the President's niece. Would mean the world to her." These words were said in a simpering tone. "Dorothy would've been fetched, you'd have been introduced, and I'd have whispered a word in her ear about her family's safety if she didn't come with us—"

Audie's heart sunk to her toes. "That's why there were two identical dresses. One for me. One for Dorothy. That's how you'd sneak her out of here, past the guards. Dressed like the kitchen maid."

Mrs. Finch cackled. "Stinky—the Commodore—planned to come back for you later. He really did. But his vision is terribly limited. No idea why I insisted on an orphan." Her words sent a chill down Audie's spine. "In the morning, Stanley will return to fetch the knitting I 'forgot' and get you out of the storeroom. Then he'll take you to the ship and you'll soon be steaming to Paris. You'll have to earn your keep en route, of course, but as an orphan you should be used to that. Once you're safely on French soil, the LeGrandes will deposit the remaining finder's fee in my bank account. And I will finally live the life I deserve." She peered at Audie. "Orphans want parents, don't they? And I'm sure the LeGrandes are lovely people. So eager for a daughter. Fifty thousand francs eager."

She pushed Audie toward the dark room. Audie caught another whiff of gardenia. The same scent she had noticed at the hotel. Her heart sank. Her stomach sank. Mrs. Finch kept talking.

"Stinky was fond of you, in his own misguided way. But really: There are so many orphans in this country. Who is going to care about one gone missing?" She gave a sharp shove and Audie tumbled inside. "Bon voyage."

Audie stumbled over something metallic, catching herself before sprawling on the floor. She cried out, "Mrs. Finch?"

The only answer she received was the ominous thud of the closing door and a key turning in the lock.

CHAPTER TWENTY-EIGHT

Done Cooking

*The cat lurked in the corner of the courtyard all afternoon. The delivery-*man with the geriatric horse had tossed her a few sardines, but hours ago. Otherwise she'd been without nourishment the entire day. The courtyard was a barren place. Not a shrub in sight. Not a twig for a bird to perch upon, not a branch for a mouse to hide beneath. The only reason the cat herself had escaped notice the entire morning and afternoon was the protection provided by the lone rain barrel. She fit nicely in the corner of the building tucked tight behind it. Ironic that this hiding place was so bereft of edibles, given that on the other side of that white wall was a kitchen, bustling with people preparing meals fit for a king. Or a president.

The cat's dearest friend had gone inside that kitchen earlier in the morning. Min knew from experience that when Audie came out, there would be some delectable tidbit to share. She ran her sandpaper tongue delicately over her mouth in anticipation. Perhaps a bit of the sea creatures she smelled in the delivery buckets. That would be tasty indeed. She licked her chops again.

The shadows had stretched long over the course of the day and were now fading with the sun. Still Audie had not exited the building. Min was a patient cat. She had occupied the interlude with an especially thorough bath, taking great care to get the notches between each of her magnificently clawed toes. With that task completed, her thoughts gave way to a time—in what she hoped would be the near future—when they would return home. A bit of occasional excitement was all well and good, but Min hoped city life was not to become a habit with Audie. The cat did not care for the odd flavor of urban mice, with that unpleasant metallic aftertaste. Give her a plump little field mouse any day, brimming with the good clean juices of clover and fresh air and healthy living.

A troubling tableau began to unfold before the cat's golden eyes. The robin's egg blue automobile glided into the courtyard. But the raven-haired man was not steering it, as he usually did. No, this time, the man who always dressed head to toe in white sat behind the wheel. As he exited the vehicle, he removed an enormous handkerchief from his vest pocket, vigorously patting his face.

A short time passed before the man and the woman, who smelled of fish, and not in a good way, stepped through the arched doorway. The same doorway that Audie had entered several hours earlier. Between them, they carried with great effort an enormous lidded bucket.

"This is not according to the plan." The man huffed and puffed as he wrestled with one handle of the bucket. "Not to plan at all."

The woman struggled equally with her handle. "Well, when opportunity knocks, I answer. Are you carrying your share of this?"

she asked. The bucket swayed wildly and it took both of them to stabilize and guide it into the backseat of the car.

"But what about Annie?" the man asked, fingers resting on the door handle.

The woman shrugged, sliding in after the bucket. "The little ash cat ran away."

The man's face clouded with confusion. "That seems so unlike her." He stood motionless, contemplating.

"Well, remember that day at the train station," the woman reminded him. "She'll be fine."

For all of his nefarious plans to exact revenge upon this auto-fanatic president for a battered pride and lost fortune, the man in white had grown fond of the orphan, had envisioned mailing her postcards from Venezuela and points south. But his capacity for caring for others was limited; thus he did not allow himself to question his companion's assertion. Nor did he allow himself to consider the dangers, toils, and snares facing an eleven-year-old girl out in the world on her own. Instead, he chose to imagine that Annie was making her way back to that woman. What was her name? Miss Margaret? Yes. Annie was no doubt halfway to Swayzee by now.

"We don't have all day," the woman snapped.

He closed the door, scuttled to the driver's seat, and off they drove.

With a bucket. But without Audie. Most certainly without Audie.

Min snapped her tail in irritation. If Audie had not departed in the robin's egg blue automobile, then where was she? Preoccupied with this thought, the usually perceptive cat failed to notice an enormous shadow pressing itself against the opposite wall as the automobile departed. Had the cat been paying attention, she might have guessed the shadow to be one cast by a great ape. In that case, she would have been only partly mistaken.

Intent upon other concerns, the cat bounded to the kitchen doorway. Underneath the aroma of horses and finned creatures she caught the whiff of something familiar. The scent of books and Sunlight soap and kinship.

The scent of her best human friend.

CHAPTER TWENTY-NINE

Cat and Mouse

Audie pounded her fists against the door. "Mrs. Finch? Mrs. Finch?" She pressed her cheek to the cold wood, resting there, gathering her wits.

No point calling out *that* name any longer. Waste of time. Audie's tingling ear had been trying to warn her of that all day. Mrs. Finch had locked her in intentionally. All because she'd seen the snippet of blue fabric under the bucket lid. Why was it there? What did it mean?

Audie's brain was as unbridled as Bimmy's curls. It was so difficult to think. To concentrate.

She pushed away from the door, blinking hard to force herself to adjust to the dark more quickly. She found a coal scuttle, flipped it upside down, and attempted to get comfortable on the makeshift chair. She wobbled to the left, overcorrected, and wobbled to the right.

"Get a grip, Audie, girl." She spoke to herself sternly. But it was hard to take herself seriously, the way her voice slipped and sloshed

154 ᠀᠊

so. Whatever was the matter? And why was the room wandering about this way and that? She wiggled her feet in her boots. The familiarity of the gold coin in each toe was small comfort.

For the second time that day, she wished she had thought ahead; even one match would've made a difference against the dark. It was unlike her to be so unprepared. Audie shook her head. No time to fret about that now.

Her stomach rumbled. If only she had been able to eat a slice of Sally Lunn cake, as had Dorothy. And where was Dorothy? Audie paused: Had she dreamed her up? Maybe. Maybe. Audie's stomach rumbled again, taking her mind in another direction.

Surely the Commodore would question her whereabouts when she didn't appear for supper. He had entrusted Audie to Mrs. Finch's care. Though he couldn't keep Audie's name straight, he would at least expect her to be returned to the hotel after her assistant soup-making responsibilities. It might take a few hours for him to put all the pieces together, but he would realize she was missing. Eventually. And come back for her. Hadn't Mrs. Finch admitted that had been his plan all along? An unpleasant notion snaked its way around Audie's swirling thoughts, chilling her through and through. She wrapped her arms around herself, facing the dreadful conclusion head-on: This visit to the White House wasn't about making soup after all, but about something more devious.

An image of Mr. Witherton's library flashed through her mind. She recalled that book on South American poisons. Undetectable poisons! Audie struggled to remain upright on her coal-scuttle chair. The soup! What if those herbs she'd chopped hadn't been marjoram or lemon thyme or parsley but hemlock or something equally sinister?

Audie's knees set to quivering like Cook's jellied calves' feet. The President would be poisoned and they could, rightfully, point the finger at Audie. She could see Mrs. Finch's thinking. Why not let an orphan take the fall? And a Wayward orphan at that? Had Audie been the blubbering type, she might have allowed herself a tear or two. But she was made of sterner stuff.

If there was a plan afoot to harm the President, Audie had best get busy trying to figure a way out of this room. She had to stop Mr. Taft from eating that soup. And she had to figure out what happened to Dorothy.

She yawned. Suddenly, she was so very, very sleepy.

Her last thought before losing consciousness was that Mrs. Finch must have put something in the tea. A decidedly nasty something.

* * *

A furry creature swished across Audie's face. She gasped, arms flailing, popping upright. Not a mouse! Or worse, a rat! She instantly calmed when her brown eyes met a pair of familiar golden ones.

"Min!" Audie's arms flew around her dear friend's neck. "Am I dreaming still?" Moments before, she had been in that sliver of space between here and not-here and it had been delicious indeed: She and her parents together, bobbing high above the most marvelous city in a rainbow-striped hot-air balloon. She had stood between her mother and her father, each resting a warm hand on her shoulder, making her feel firmly grounded in spite of the altitude. Though great was Audie's pleasure at seeing Min, fragments of that precious dream clung to her like sticky cobwebs, cobwebs from which she did not wish to be disentangled. As the last strands peeled away, the longing for her beloved parents nipped at her heart like a snapping turtle.

That wasn't the only pain she felt. Her neck was complaining vociferously about her having used the coal scuttle as a pillow. She whimpered in the most unbecoming manner as she attempted to unkink it, wincing as she rubbed. It might never be straight again. Then she stopped in mid-massage. "Say, Min. How on earth did you get in here?"

Min sniffed at Audie's face and hands, assessing her ability for travel. The cat surmised that her friend had consumed something that had made her ill. Sleepy. She sniffed again. It appeared to be largely cleared from her system. Travel seemed a safe and reasonable option.

Min meowed.

"The soup!" It was all coming back to Audie. "Is it tomorrow, Min? Is the President—?" She jumped up. "How did you get in? Can I get out the same way?" Questions skittered around in her brain like popcorn kernels in hot oil.

Min padded to a corner of the room to point out a mouse hole, enlarged through patient and persistent scratching, which had provided her entrance.

"Clever cat," Audie complimented her. "But I'll never get through there." And it would take forever to carve it into an Audie-sized hole. Time was a precious and evaporating commodity. Propelled by a sense of urgency, Audie paced around the room, searching for some kind of useful tool. She picked up an old broom head and dropped it back to the floor. Likewise she discarded a percolator lid, an empty lard tin, and a canning jar lifter. "What a worthless lot of trash!" She threw a colander against the door.

Min sat, calmly cleaning her right forepaw throughout the entire frantic demonstration. When the colander finished bouncing and had come to a rest, the cat stood, shook her head daintily, and padded toward the door. She whipped her lithe tail, then raised herself on her hind two legs and batted at the doorknob.

"I've tried, Min." Audie resumed her search for a useful tool. She uncovered an eggbeater missing its handle and thrust it into the air like a sword. "It's locked."

Min continued batting at the door. She meowed. Insistently.

"All right. All right." Audie dropped the broken kitchen utensil and stomped across the room. "I'll show you. It won't open. I tried a hundred times last night." She reached for the knob. "See?"

It turned. It clicked.

The door swung open.

Is it possible that a cat could mysteriously open a door that was heretofore locked? We leave it to you to judge. But we do provide this gentle reminder: Min is one remarkable cat.

Audie stared at her friend. "You're a magician!"

Min ducked her head modestly. Then she darted out into the hallway. They had much to accomplish and precious little time.

There would be ample opportunity for Audie to sing Min's praises later.

CHAPTER THIRTY

Run for Your Life

Still a bit wobbly from whatever potion Mrs. Finch had slipped into the tea, Audie could only run a few steps before she had to pause and lean against a wall. Min growled a warning.

"I know." Audie rubbed her forehead. "Give me a chance to gather my wits."

Another low growl.

And then Audie heard the reason for Min's alarm. Footsteps. Heavy footsteps. Fear threatened to turn her into an ice sculpture right there in the darkened back hallway of the White House basement. Audie attempted to whisper encouragement to Min but her mouth was as dry as Miss Maisie's bath talc. Min wrapped her tail around Audie's leg and tugged, signaling the girl to follow.

With practiced care, Audie stepped ever so silently. *One, two, three, four.* Finally, her steps brought her to a small niche into which had been pushed an old armoire. While the footsteps pounded in rhythm with her heart, Audie painstakingly opened the door—which thankfully did not creak—and climbed inside. Min slipped in, too, and curled up at her feet. Audie was grateful for the company but hated to think that she had placed her dear friend in grave danger.

As the footsteps crept closer, Audie pulled the door shut. The hinges were askew, leaving a slit of light between the two doors. This provided a sight line into the hallway.

All too soon, a man turned a corner. Audie had a clear view of his face: He was a bellman at the Ardmore! The one the Commodore often spoke to. What on earth was he doing here? He glanced over his shoulder, clearly nervous. But why? Then she realized that he was standing stock-still but the sound of footsteps could still be heard. Heavier footsteps. She edged her way to the back of the armoire, reaching down to stroke Min's back for comfort.

The bellman started up again, making a direct line for the room from which Audie had recently escaped. He muttered something when he found the door ajar. "Annie?" he whispered. "Where are you?"

The tone of his voice caused Audie to press herself more firmly to the back of the armoire. She turned her head to the side, half afraid to look, but more afraid not to.

"Come out, come out, wherever you are."

Audie heard the man stumble against the assorted wreckage of the storeroom. He must have barked his shin on something for he issued the most creative string of oaths.

It flashed through Audie's mind that he might be preoccupied enough for her to make a run for it. But something held her back.

And that was a good thing. Because the creator of the heavier footfalls had now rounded the corner himself. Audie stifled a gasp to see a man of such brawn and burliness. Her heart began to beat double-time. There would be no escape from such a brute.

Instead of lurching toward the armoire, ripping off the door, and dragging Audie out to some unimaginable end, the brute followed the bellman into the storeroom. Audie heard a scream of surprise and then the undeniable sounds of a scuffle.

It was over in an instant. Audie opened her eyes and peeked out in time to see the brute toss the bellman over his shoulder as if he were a baby. The bellman moaned quietly. "I didn't do anything," he sniveled.

"Tell zat to zee polizia," said the brute. And with that, they were gone.

Audie was a girl as full of spunk and courage as the next, but it was several minutes before her legs stopped trembling and she could climb down out of the armoire.

"Do you know what that was all about, Min?" she asked.

Min shook herself in reply before meowing at her friend.

"I know. Time is running out." Audie took one last deep breath to steady herself. "Like Cook says, talk doesn't fry eggs. Let's go."

CHAPTER THIRTY-ONE

Incriminating Evidence

Sans hat and coat, Audie shivered as she ran out into the first day of the new year. Min bounded ahead, away from the White House.

"Min, where are you going? Come back!" Having recently escaped capture by both the bellman and the brute, Audie was not ready to face the next phase of her adventure alone.

Ignoring Audie's pleas, Min dashed out of the kitchen courtyard, and, with a twitch of her tail, was smartly around the corner and gone.

Audie started to follow but froze as she caught sight of a familiar profile. Cypher! She wiggled behind a shrub and held her breath. The last thing she wanted was to be discovered by anyone in cahoots with the Commodore.

Oddly, instead of entering the courtyard and continuing on through the kitchen, Cypher disappeared around the far corner of the White House. Pretty brazen of him to be traipsing around the national grounds like that. Audie could only hope that his brazenness would be rewarded with a long spell in the clink.

Once Cypher had vanished from view, it seemed the more sensible course of action to head in the opposite direction. Audie batted her way out from behind the shrub, pulling off dead twigs and leaves as she ran toward the Ellipse. Her heart lifted when she saw the flag flying proudly above the White House. Surely if any ill had befallen President Taft, the flag would be flying at half-staff.

"Paper! Getcher paper!" A clear voice pealed through the cold morning air like a church bell. It carried a note of familiarity that made Audie turn.

"Juice!" She flew to her friend.

"Are you trying to catch pneumonia?" He shrugged out of his coat and threw it over her shoulders. "It's winter, in case you haven't noticed."

"Is the President all right?"

"Right as rain." Juice showed her the front-page headlines. "Ready to host the New Year's Day reception."

Audie secured Juice's coat around her. "That's all the news there is about him?"

Juice turned to sell a paper to a man with whiskers so full and curly that he resembled a lion. Then he turned back to Audie. "What more would there be?" he asked.

"His niece is missing," she said.

"Go on with you."

Audie grabbed his arm. "More than missing. Kidnapped." Lightheaded, she wobbled against her friend.

"Whoa, there." Juice steadied her. "You're not going to faint again, are you?"

A nice faint might be just the ticket. Take leave of her senses and responsibilities for a precious interval and let others handle things. Events had taken a turn that was beyond her capability, of that she was convinced. Being trapped in a storeroom was one thing; a kidnapping was quite another. Such situations were best left to professionals.

Audie could envision explaining everything to the police, or the Secret Service men. Before two words had left her mouth, they would arrest her for being an accomplice. Or worse! She should have stayed back at Miss Maisie's. Why had she thought *she* could make a difference in the world? She was only an orphan. A well-read one, perhaps, but a powerless orphan all the same. Audie grappled mightily with the consequences of having spent so much time with her nose in a book. Clearly, that habit had left her ill equipped to deal with the realities of life.

Audie inhaled deeply. She was practical enough to concede that point. But she'd come too far to give up now. She was many things, most of them flawed, but she was not a quitter. Things were far from splendid, so this episode in her life was far from over.

"And I know who took her." Audie shivered. No wonder Mrs. Finch had asked the deliveryman to leave the turtle bucket. It was big enough to hold someone Audie's size. Someone like Dorothy.

Juice peered at her. "You don't look too good. Maybe you best come with me. Daddy Dub can make you some tea." He reached for her arm.

"No! No tea." She shook him off.

The look he gave her was pure bewilderment.

"I drank something odd last night. A sleeping potion. Not on purpose. The people who took Dorothy drugged me. Or at least one of them did." She should have known Mrs. Finch wasn't English by the way she held those needles. No Englishwoman would knit in the Continental style. And her accent wasn't even that convincing.

Juice's brow wrinkled. He studied Audie for a full minute, as if weighing something. Making a decision. After the minute passed, he gave a sharp nod, then put his finger to his lips. "Best tone it down a bit," he said, indicating all the people milling around. "If what you say is true—"

"It's true!" Audie stamped her foot.

"Okay. Okay." Juice held up his hands. "What we need is a plan. Hard to hatch one out here in the freezing cold. With all these ears listening in."

Audie sniffled. He did have a point there. "Oh, all right. But we have to be quick about it. There's not much time!"

They ran to the White House stables and found Daddy Dub. He was going through an old chest in one of the empty stalls. He eased himself onto a stool, and asked Audie to tell him everything that had happened. She thought she might explode with impatience. Who knew where Dorothy had been taken? Each tick of the minute hand worked to their disadvantage.

Audie explained her concerns about the press of time, but Daddy Dub shushed her. "Good thinking takes good time." He patted his bony thighs. "Start at the beginning and don't leave one thing out."

Audie did as asked, only stopping when Daddy Dub or Juice asked a question. She confessed that she had misled them about the relationship between her and the Commodore. "He's not my uncle," she admitted. "He chose me to help him with a mission. I didn't know it was going to be anything like this." She covered her face with her hands.

"Is that everything?" Daddy Dub asked.

She nodded. She decided against mentioning the brute and the bellman because she didn't know what role they played in the kidnapping. And she was half afraid that mentioning the brute might dissuade Juice and his grandfather from coming to her aid.

"I think I know who I should talk to." Daddy Dub stood up, pulling a blanket out of the old chest. "First I've got to cover Murphy up," he said. "Sounded like he was catching cold." When he shook out the blanket, a cascade of silken rosettes spilled onto the straw-covered floor.

Audie reached her hand up to touch her head. It had seemed like forever ago that Beatrice had fixed her hair. With the stimulating events of the past several hours, hair accessories had been the last thing on her mind. She unpinned the Commodore's rosette and compared it to one from the chest. "These look so much alike." She turned over the other rosette, running her fingers along the intricate folds, studying the stitching. Stamped on the back were the initials: CC.

Daddy Dub also compared the two rosettes. "See how these folds are as sharp and tiny as can be?" He pointed to the frilled edge. "That's the trademark of Crutchfield Creations. Used to be the only man President Roosevelt would buy his livery fol-de-rols from. That Mr. Crutchfield was a mighty rich man. Mighty rich. Yes, sir."

"Miss Maisie said he was the richest man in Swayzee. Maybe in Indiana," Audie added.

"I expect that's so." The old man nodded. "Near about everyone who was anyone ordered from Crutchfield. Horse people, that is."

Audie's left ear began to tingle. Though she was only eleven and not overly concerned with monetary matters, it didn't take financial know-how to reach the conclusion that, with the coming of the automobile, perhaps the Commodore was not so rich. At least, not any longer. And if he was not so rich because of the automobile, he was probably none too happy with President Taft.

"And he blames it on the President," she said aloud, sliding her rosette into her pocket.

"What?" Juice asked.

"Likely so." Daddy Dub quickly tracked Audie's train of thought. He picked up a rucksack, and filled it with an odd assortment of items.

Audie pressed her hand to her pounding heart. "Oh, poor Dorothy." It was difficult to fathom, but it was now apparent that the Commodore had thought to exact his revenge on the President by kidnapping his niece.

"Get me my coat and hat, there, will you, Juice?" Daddy Dub handed Audie the rucksack. The action reminded her that she had left her own rucksack behind at the White House. "Dorothy's going to be fine." He winked at Audie. "She's got us on her side, doesn't she?"

Audie wasn't certain that a newsboy, an orphan, and a fragile old man made much of a rescue team, but Daddy Dub exuded such confidence that she couldn't disagree with him. "Yes, she does."

"Don't you fret." Daddy Dub put out the lantern with a hiss. "That Commodore's going to be real sorry he tangled with us."

CHAPTER THIRTY-TWO

Plan B

The Commodore sulked in the overstuffed club chair. The girl had put up such a fuss when they removed her from the bucket, a fuss that resulted in a black spot on his white suit coat. A permanent stain, no doubt.

And it was all Elva's fault.

"None of this was according to plan," he reminded her for the umpteenth time.

Elva gritted her teeth before answering. "As I told you before, when opportunity knocks, we must answer." She lavished a piece of toast with creamy golden butter, and then took a dainty bite. "Besides, this is much more sophisticated than what you had in mind. And far less complicated." She dabbed her mouth with a linen napkin.

Less complicated! Less complicated! He had laid out a blueprint for stashing Annie in the old storeroom at the White House—Stanley'd been well paid to recover her and send her back to Swayzee—borrowing Dorothy for a few hours before returning her to the bosom of her family, and adding a goodly sum of American dollars to his pocket all within twenty-four hours.

Now, they'd been stuck with Dorothy since the prior afternoon, and the ransom note hadn't been delivered. Hadn't been sent! But the Commodore knew he would only suffer further if he vexed Elva. "Less complicated, perhaps, but not as well thought out."

"What's to think out? We deliver the note and get our money." She finished chewing. "Easy as pie, Stinky."

The Commodore exhaled sharply. "I've asked you not to call me that."

Elva smirked. "Easy as pie. *Millard.*"

He smoothed out his moustache. "So how are we going to deliver the note, *Elva?*" He had her there. These things took planning. Calculations! And flair. It had been a sheer stroke of genius on his part to come up with such a novel way to deliver a ransom note: words carved on the inside of one of the turtle shells used to make the President's Terrapin Soup.

The Commodore now allowed himself to bask in the scene he'd long envisioned: The soup-filled shell being carried up on a silver serving tray, which would be placed in front of the President by a black-jacketed waiter wearing white gloves. While he was engaged in chitchat with his tablemates, sip by sip, the President would dip ever closer to the chilling message: *Now Dorothy's in the soup. Wait for instructions.* The Commodore was warmed by a wave of self-satisfaction at such clever phrasing.

Elva clinked her teacup against the saucer, bumping the Commodore out of his pleasant daydream and into the present painful reality of having to abandon that splendid scheme. It really had been remarkable. Grand. But all gone to ashes because of Elva's impulses. And now Annie had deserted him in his hour of need. Ungrateful girl.

"What are we to do about delivering the note?"

Elva polished off the rest of her toast, licking the crumbs from her fingers. "We will attend the New Year's reception today and you will slip the note to the President while you shake his hand."

Every New Year's Day since George Washington's time, the sitting president had opened the White House to greet as many members of the public who were willing to wait in a very long line on a cold winter day. It was said that, in 1907, President Theodore Roosevelt shook over ten thousand hands; it was thought that Taft would shake perhaps half that number at his first New Year's Day reception. Sadly, President Taft was what the common folk called "unpopular." As has been mentioned previously, there is no accounting for taste.

The Commodore stared at her. "That is your plan?" Elva was going to be the death of him. Why had he ever thought involving her in this caper would be a good idea? "I can hardly hand the President a ransom note! We'll be snatched into jail quicker than you can crack an egg." He rubbed his temple. "Good heavens, Elva. What are you thinking?"

Her skirts rustled as she sat upright. "Stink—I mean, Millard. Don't get yourself so agitated. When you get agitated, you prevent yourself from seeing possibilities. Of course, I didn't mean we'd hand the note over, right there in front of everyone." She caressed the fat curl that dangled over her right ear, batting her eyes all the while. "You'll pin it to his chest."

The Commodore felt all the blood vessels in his head constrict. She was going to give him a stroke. A stroke! "I'll pin it to his chest?" The words were as distasteful in his mouth as cod liver oil.

"Oh, Millard, my dear. You are such a card." Elva stood, shaking her skirt as she did so. "Allow me to demonstrate." She slid the ransom note from the breakfast table, and folded it into a tight square. Then she pressed the pin on the backing of a rosette through the paper, and affixed both rosette and note to the Commodore's vest. "Like so."

"The Secret Service will be on me like ticks!" The Commodore patted his sweating forehead. "You've lost your senses, Elva. You truly have."

"Dear St—Millard." She smiled. "The President will be delighted to receive a gift from a loyal constituent." She pulled a letter from her bodice, unfolded it, and waved it in front him. "This is from Teddy, vouching that he knows you and sending his best wishes to Taft."

"President Roosevelt wrote a letter like that for me?" The pleasure from such knowledge boosted the Commodore's spirits considerably.

Elva rolled her eyes. "No. He did not write this. I did. And forged his signature." She returned the letter to her bodice for safekeeping. "Honestly, sometimes you are utterly innocent."

"Well, I've never done anything like this before," the Commodore grumbled. His lower lip protruded in a pitiful pout.

Elva rustled across the room, removing her hat from the dresser top. "That's all the more reason to trust me, isn't it?" She secured the outlandish *chapeau* to her pomaded hair with a diamond-tipped hat pin. She gave the hat a pat, then motioned for the Commodore to assist her with her coat. "We'd best be going. The doors close at two o'clock and we don't want to be left standing in the cold."

"Shouldn't we check on . . ." The Commodore looked over his shoulder, as if someone might be listening in on their conversation. "You know." He slipped Elva's black velveteen coat over her shoulders.

She arched an eyebrow. "She's not going anywhere. And besides, Stanley took her a breakfast tray. She'll be fine until we return." Elva buttoned her coat, humming "Frère Jacques" to herself. Stanley should have Annie in hand by now, on his way to the SS *Parisian*. Soon, soon, all those lovely francs would be deposited in her bank account and she would be on a journey herself, far, far away from Millard and Stanley and orphans of every kind.

The Commodore buttoned up his own overcoat, and placed his derby carefully atop his white locks. "You know more about these things than I do." He offered his arm and Elva Finch took it. Together, they strolled out of the room. They squeezed into the elevator with an astonishingly large man accompanied by the tiniest of young women. The Commodore tipped his hat to the young lady.

She nodded. "*Jó napot kívánok!* Good day," she said. The Commodore thought her slight accent charming. But her companion was a trifle intimidating.

He was relieved to exit the elevator and pass through the lobby to stand under the Ardmore Hotel's grand awning, where he and Elva awaited the arrival of the robin's egg blue touring car.

As they stood on the sidewalk, the partners in crime were

unaware of a well-nourished chocolate-striped feline watching them while hidden behind one of the hotel's immense flower urns. The two humans were so engrossed in conversation that they also did not notice the cat, eye level with their stylish kid-leather shoes—Elva Finch's a soft dove gray and the Commodore's spit-polished black—inch closer and closer, as if to pounce. But she did not pounce. She sniffed, taking in the faint aroma of horse and hay, faint because the aroma was not fresh. It spoke of scents from years past. There wasn't much time to take in such smells because shortly a long, lean automobile pulled up to the curb and the pair disappeared inside and were gone. Fortunately, the cat's sense of smell was acute and her vocabulary of aromas was large. It hadn't taken long to identify what she'd smelled. She knew where she needed to go, what she needed to do.

Min leapt into action, running back toward President's Park. Most specifically, toward the White House stables. As she bounded across the lawn, she did her best to avoid the gathering citizens, already lining up for their annual chance to shake the President's hand. The cat zigged this way and zagged that to avoid clumsy feet. Her tail dodged several near misses, but on she ran.

As luck would have it, the objects of her mission were advancing in her very direction.

"Min!" Audie ran to her friend and scooped her into a hug. "Where did you disappear to?" Juice caught up to them. Daddy Dub, hobbled by his advanced years and bum knee, lagged a significant ways behind.

"This is my friend Min," Audie said.

Juice grinned. "We've had the pleasure of meeting."

The cat purred and rubbed her head on the underside of Audie's chin. And then she did something surprising. She nipped the tender flesh at Audie's neck.

"Ouch!" Audie was so startled, she released her grip and Min thumped to the ground.

"*Rowr. Rowr.*" Min's tail whipped impatiently.

"Looks like she wants us to follow her," Juice said.

Audie and Juice chased after Min in fits and starts. They had to hurry to keep up with the cat, but pace themselves so as not to lose Daddy Dub. Progress was also slowed by all the citizens lining up for the New Year's reception. After a few blocks, Min dashed up to a brick building, found some kind of cat-sized entrance, and disappeared inside.

Audie ran to the front door and tugged. "Locked."

Juice found a stick nearby and gave a whack. The padlock held firm.

Daddy Dub soon reached them, panting. "These are the Ardmore's old stables." He wiped at his forehead with the back of his hand. "Looks like the hotel's selling the building." He pointed at a FOR SALE sign. "I bet it's empty."

Audie's left ear felt as if a mosquito were trapped inside, it was buzzing that crazily. "I don't think it's empty," she said slowly. "I think this is where they're keeping Dorothy." That had to be why Min led them here. "We have to get her out," she said. "Before the Commodore comes back." It was painful to even say that name. Though she had been dubious about him from the start, she had never dreamed he would cause anyone harm. Least of all two innocent girls.

"Hold your horses, Audie." Juice put his hand on her arm. "We don't know who all's in there."

Audie chewed her lip. Juice was right. Perhaps someone was inside, guarding Dorothy. Maybe Cypher? Or maybe the brute?

"Here's what we'll do." Daddy Dub rubbed his grizzled chin. "You children keep an eye here. My friend runs a café a few blocks away. I'll go up there, ask to use the telephone, and fetch that help I talked about."

"But—" Audie feared there might not be time to wait.

"I'll be back before you can say Jack Robinson." Daddy Dub hobbled down the sidewalk. "Stay put."

"Yes, sir!" Juice called after him.

Daddy Dub was scarcely out of sight when Audie grabbed Juice by the arm.

"Follow me."

"Daddy Dub said stay put."

"I know she's in there, Juice." Audie stared into her friend's eyes. "And I don't know if we have time to wait any longer. Do you? Really?"

Juice returned her gaze and then sighed. "Whatever you say."

They hurried to scout the building's perimeter. Pausing on the far side, Audie pointed. "If we could get up to those windows, we could look inside. See what we're up against." Our quick-minded heroine also deduced that those windows would likely have to serve as their entry point as well, owing to the enormous padlock on the front doors.

Juice stretched himself up tall. "Even if I boosted you, you couldn't see in."

Each second that passed ate into the likelihood of rescuing Dorothy. Audie glanced around. "I've got an idea." She pointed at a horse and buggy across the way.

"I hope you're not thinking what I think you're thinking." Juice tugged on his cap. "They still hang horse thieves around here."

"Come on." Audie wiggled out of her right boot. "I only hope you have your grandfather's touch with horses."

Juice groaned. But he did just what Audie asked.

CHAPTER THIRTY-THREE

A Meow in the Dark

Dorothy snugged the rough wool blanket around her shoulders. It was cold in this place. Cold and dark. She shifted to find a more comfortable position on the wood floor, trying to avoid the sharp ends of dried hay straws. Her feet accidentally knocked over the glass of milk that horrid bellman had left. What was his name? Stanley? If she got out of here, she was certainly going to remember that name. He would regret his involvement in this despicable affair.

She rolled away from the spilled milk so she wouldn't get wet, knocking over the untouched breakfast tray. On a good day, oatmeal was something she could only manage to swallow down. And whatever they'd drugged her with had left her feeling sick at her stomach. Not one bite of that porridge would pass between her lips. Besides, she could not be assured it wasn't drugged as well. She shifted herself gently, careful not to jog her head, which felt like it might wobble right off her neck.

With every fiber of her being, she forced all terrifying thoughts to a far corner of her mind. Why was she here? What did they want with her? Uncle William and Aunt Nellie would've been worried sick when she didn't show up for supper. What must they be thinking now? Of course, Charlie wouldn't have noticed she'd gone. If he had, his only thought would have been: *Goody. One fewer tiresome cousin. No more charades.*

Dorothy sniffled, running her tied hands under her nose. She thought about the kitchen girl. Annie. What had she thought when she came back with the parsley to find Dorothy missing? Of course, she was only a servant. She would have accepted whatever story that awful cook fed her. Dorothy was confident of one thing. Annie wasn't part of this kidnapping plot. There'd been something so honest and true about her. Under other circumstances, they might have been friends. Had she not been hired help.

Something rustled nearby. Dorothy froze. Please don't let it be a rat. Please. That would be unbearable. She pulled her knees up to her chest, shrinking as small as possible. Less likely that the rat would crawl over her that way.

Another rustle.

Dorothy could not remain silent. "Is someone there?" Her voice caught in her throat like a wad of cotton. She coughed. Tried again. "Anyone?" Held her breath, awaiting a reply.

It came in the form of a meow. And following that meow, around the wooden half wall, slipped a cat. Dorothy wasn't sure why, but she burst into tears. The first tears shed since the onset of her ordeal.

"Hello, puss." She patted the floor next to her clumsily. The cat padded closer, sniffing at the spilled milk and then at the rope tightly knotted around the girl's wrists.

"I'm so glad to see you!" If there were rats in this horrid place, this tabby looked capable of dispatching them with ease. Dorothy wiggled her fingers and the cat sniffed at those, too, then padded closer to wash away the tears on her cheek with a sandpapery tongue. "Thank you, kitty. Thank you."

"Meow." The cat tilted its head, as if trying to communicate something to Dorothy. Its golden eyes sent waves of comfort and hope washing over the girl. Then it turned and darted away, and, with a flick of a tail, left her alone, all alone, once again.

* CHAPTER THIRTY-FOUR *

New Year's Day

It had pained Audie greatly to part with that gold coin. Not that she cared for money, mind you. But it did hurt to give up one of the two remaining keepsakes from her parents. It could not be helped. The owner drove a hard bargain. "Do you want the steed or not?" he'd asked, scratching his head under his filthy cap.

Audie wanted to say "not," but the scabbed and bony horse clearly needed rescuing as desperately as she needed its help rescuing Dorothy. She pressed the gold coin to her heart, then handed it over to the rapscallion. She was certain her sweet mother would approve of this expenditure.

He sniggered as he handed her the reins. "Not much of a horse trader, are you?"

With every ounce of pride she could muster, Audie took the horse's bridle and tugged him over to where Juice waited.

"Did you steal him?" Juice asked.

"No. Bought him fair and square." That was a lie; a true horse trader like Daddy Dub would say the horse wasn't worth the price Audie had paid. But the horse—she would call him Samuel after her father—looked at her so gratefully that Audie quickly moved on to a discussion of the rescue plan. What was money after all? Merely a burden unless put to good use.

* * *

"Hurry up!" Juice tugged at the horse's bridle to get the animal situated precisely under the window. "This horse looks like nothing but trouble."

"Samuel understands working for the greater good," Audie said calmly. "He is a tremendously wise creature."

Juice looked the animal over. "Wise creature, my behind," he muttered under his breath. With a final bit of maneuvering, he got the horse properly placed. "Okay, okay. Climb aboard."

Audie grabbed hold of the harness breech strap and pulled herself up. Juice lent a hand getting her hind end up high enough to straddle Samuel's back. At the same time, Audie raised her right leg and placed her booted foot under her. She repeated the same action with her left side and was now crouching, froglike, atop the steed. Samuel balked at the unfamiliar weight.

"Hey, there. *Shuh, shuh, shuh.*" Juice held the bridle tight, speaking calming nonsense words to the horse, stroking gently right between its eyes.

"On the count of three," Audie said.

"I've got him. He'll be fine. Won't you, horse?" More stroking between the eyes.

"His name is Samuel," Audie said.

Juice spit. "He'll be fine. Won't you, Samuel?" An unlikelier horse hero could not be found in the entire city.

"One, two—" On that last word, Audie pushed herself to stand, teetering on horseflesh. "Three!"

"Hold on!" Juice encouraged.

Audie wiggled her feet, feeling the remaining gold coin under her left toes and taking confidence from it. She steadied her breath and her legs, leaned toward the window, and peered inside. It was as dark as Cypher's heart but she could make out a dozen stalls, nearly all of their doors hanging ajar.

A motion caught her eye. "Min!" She tapped on the window and the cat turned its head toward her. "Is the coast clear?"

"You think that cat's going to answer you?" Juice asked.

"Yes." Audie kept her eyes on her feline friend. All seemed quiet. Deserted. No sign of Cypher. Or anyone else. She shivered at the thought of the brute.

There was no sign of Dorothy, either.

"I hope we have the right place." Audie shifted her weight to get more evenly balanced. She scanned the room inside again, carefully, thoughtfully. Maybe she'd missed something. But what? She squinted and focused intently.

Wait. All the stall doors were opened. Except for one. She gripped the window frame and shoved. Hard. "Oh, dear." She tottered like a tightrope walker about to fall off the tightrope.

"Hang on!" Juice caught one of her flailing hands to help right her.

"I'm okay. This window's stuck." She pushed again and the window budged. Push. Budge. Push. Budge. Finally, it slid all the way up in the wooden sash. "I'm going in," she whispered over her shoulder.

"Daddy Dub's going to read us the riot act." Juice shook his head. "I hope you're doing the right thing."

"I am." Audie shinnied herself up on the sill. "Now keep an eye out. And run if there's trouble." She squirmed to a sitting position, ready to push through the opening. It didn't look like too long a drop.

"I'm not going anywhere unless it's for the police. You've got five minutes in there," Juice warned.

"Deal." And with that, Audie disappeared.

She landed with a hard thump, but muffled her cry with knuckle to mouth. Shaking out her skirt and her legs, she padded toward the closed stall door, heart pounding loud enough to be heard across town. Min appeared next to her, then with a single easy bound, lit atop the stall's half wall.

"Who's there?" a small, shaky voice wobbled out to her.

"Dorothy?" Audie called.

"Annie!" Dorothy cried. "You're all right! I'm so relieved!"

Audie fiddled with the latch on the door and swung it wide. "We've got to get you out of here and fast." She removed the dried straw from Dorothy's clothing, looking her over for injuries. "Can you run?"

Dorothy nodded. "As soon as I get untied."

Audie reached into her coat pocket. Actually, Juice's coat pocket. Thankfully, the boy carried a small but excruciatingly sharp pocket-knife to cut the twine that bound his paper bundles. Audie was certain Juice wouldn't mind her using it on Dorothy's ropes. She pressed on the brass bee decoration and a blade snicked out. "Hold still." She sawed the blade back and forth, back and forth, across the coarse rope fibers. Min batted at the bits that curled to the floor.

"Hurry!" Dorothy urged. "I don't know when they're coming back."

"I've almost got it." A few more sawing motions and the fibers released their hold on one another and on Dorothy's wrists. Audie reached for Dorothy's newly freed hands and tugged the other girl to her feet. They darted back the way she'd come. Audie came to an abrupt stop. It was one thing to drop down from that window. It was far too high to climb out.

"Juice!" she hissed. "Are you there?"

Dorothy squeezed her hand as they awaited an answer. None came.

"Juice?" Audie called again, a bit louder this time.

"I'm here." His voice was muffled by the distance it traveled from the ground outside.

Audie confessed to having failed to plan an exit.

Then she heard another voice. "I told you to stay put." Daddy Dub was not pleased.

"I know. And I'm sorry." Audie glanced at Dorothy. "But I have what we were after."

"All right, then. All right." Something in Daddy Dub's voice slowed the quick step of Audie's heart. "I've sent Juice to my friend's café. He'll be back in a flash with a hacksaw."

"Is the other help coming?" Audie asked.

Daddy Dub grunted. "Couldn't reach my friend. Got some gob with hay for brains instead. We gotta get to the White House."

Audie squeezed Dorothy's hand. "We'll get you home, don't worry."

Dorothy didn't say anything. The girls quietly made their way toward the front of the stables. By the time they got there, they could hear the metal rasp of the hacksaw chewing on the padlock. It seemed a day passed before Juice cheered and the door swung open.

"Don't ever do that to me again." Juice tugged his cap lower across his forehead. "You were in there forever!"

"Miss Dorothy Taft, meet Juice. And his grandfather Daddy Dub." Out in the light, Audie took stock of the rescued girl. Her face was white as bleached muslin, except for the faint purple shadow of a bruise on her cheekbone. "Are you sure you can walk?"

"Walk?" Dorothy tugged the rough blanket around her shoulders. "Right now, I am so happy, I could fly."

"Attagirl." Juice patted her shoulder. Then he looked at Audie with a question in his eyes. "Where to?"

"Where else?" Audie exchanged glances with Daddy Dub. "The White House."

"What about Samuel?" Juice asked.

"Samuel?" Dorothy asked.

Audie quickly explained about the valiant old steed.

"Seems like I best find Samuel a home next to Murphy and Selma for now." Daddy Dub motioned for Juice to heft him up onto the horse's back. "You three make your way to our stables, too, you hear? Then we'll go on from there."

"Yes, sir."

Audie took Daddy Dub's rucksack from Juice, slipping the strap over her shoulder before wrapping her arm around Dorothy's waist. They began to tear along, with Min and Juice hot on their kid-leather heels.

Within a few minutes, they were hemmed in by throngs of handshake-seeking citizens. Their numbers had trebled since Audie and Juice had passed earlier. They were salmon swimming upstream in their effort to meet up with Daddy Dub. Audie surveyed the situation, tugging Dorothy toward a hole in the crowd.

Then she stopped, jerked Dorothy back, and motioned frantically to Juice. "Bees and bonnets!" She pointed to the Commodore, a black woolen coat over his customary white garb, and Mrs. Finch, wearing a dreadful hat on which was perched an entire stuffed bird of some sort.

"We can't let them see *her*." Audie nodded at Dorothy. She shook off the dual disgust at seeing the pair and at Mrs. Finch's grotesque hat. "Time for evasive action." She drew her friends into a nook behind a gigantic evergreen shrub and divvied up the items Daddy Dub had packed in the rucksack. Within minutes, Juice looked a proper footman, Dorothy a kitchen maid, complete with white kerchief and apron, and Audie a newsboy. Thankfully, her hair fit neatly under Juice's cap. And his knickers were only slightly too long.

They each straightened up their costumes and took a last look. "Ready?" Audie asked.

"For what?" Dorothy said.

Audie tugged on her cap and grinned. "Why, to shake the President's hand, of course."

"We're supposed to meet up with Daddy Dub," Juice warned. "We gave our word."

Dorothy got a quizzical look. "Why can't I just go in?"

"We can't do either thing. Not right now." Audie pointed to her left ear. "Because of the buzzing."

"Buzzing?" Juice squinted at her.

"You mean like an earache?" asked Dorothy.

"I can't explain it." Audie cast an imploring look at each of her companions. "I must ask you to trust me."

"I do," said Dorothy.

"We do," said Juice.

They returned to the New Year's reception crowd.

"We'll never get in if we go to the back of line," Juice pointed out. "Not when it goes clear across Seventeenth Street."

Dorothy grabbed their coat sleeves. "Let's find a motherly type and blend in."

"As easy as that?" Audie asked. Juice pulled at his collar.

"As easy as that." Dorothy winked at the two of them. "Now, buck up!"

"That's one sassy gal," Juice said.

"Who would've imagined?" Audie smiled.

"No one in my family, that's for certain." Dorothy tugged on her kerchief, causing Audie to blink. In that instant, Dorothy carried the look of a pirate about her.

Audie shook that ridiculous image out of her head and followed Dorothy as she weaseled her way closer to the front. But not too close to the Commodore and Mrs. Finch. Audie pointed to a puffed-up woman wearing a Daughters of the American Revolution sash, who was distracted by the mischief making of her two small sons. Dorothy waved her friends in behind her, acting as if that was where they belonged. No one seemed to notice that they'd cut in. At least, no one commented about it.

The trio was so intent on keeping a careful eye on the Commodore and Mrs. Finch that they did not notice the duo in line some yards behind them.

"Minden rendben," said the tiny woman. "All is well." The gigantic man with her merely nodded.

As they nudged their way in line behind the distracted mother, Audie looked at Dorothy with new admiration. She had some spunk, that was certain. Even after all she'd been through. She leaned in to Audie, sharing an observation that planted the seed of a plan. "They're not very good kidnappers," Dorothy said. "I overheard the bellman, Stanley, say that they hadn't delivered the ransom note yet."

Audie reflected on the last time she'd seen Stanley. She doubted he would be able to assist the Commodore in delivering a ransom note. But this she kept from her friends.

"Hard to figure why they're standing in this long line." Juice shook his head.

"If only we knew what they were up to." Audie tipped her head toward the Commodore and Mrs. Finch. Audie was too far behind to overhear any conversation.

"Way this line is moving, we've got ourselves some time to work that out." Juice stamped his feet to warm them. "Going to get frostbit at this rate."

"Think warm thoughts," Audie encouraged. "Pretend it's summer."

Juice shivered. "My imagination's not that good."

Slowly, they shuffled closer and closer to their objective. Soon they would trudge up to the north portico. Across the threshold and on to the Red Room, where the certainly weary President waited, right hand outstretched, to shake hands with his compatriots. Step. Step. Step. And only a yard or so in front of them in line, also marched the Commodore and Mrs. Finch. Step. Step. Step.

With each inch forward, Audie's mind raced to work out how being in this receiving line might fit into the Commodore's plan. She noticed that he patted his vest pocket frequently. What was in there that he was keeping such careful track of? Might it be the not-yet-delivered ransom note?

Though Audie had merely skimmed it—the language was painfully dry—she had partaken of Mr. Witherton's small section on the law. Had she been more studious, she might now be able to understand the finer points of certain crimes, such as kidnapping. For example, our heroine mused, without the ransom note, could what had happened to Dorothy technically, legally, be called a kidnapping? Audie experienced a wave of bitter disappointment in herself for not having paid closer attention to those books. That was a situation she would remedy without delay upon her return home.

Turning back to the situation at hand, she posed the question to her comrades. "Without a note, is there a kidnapping?"

Juice shrugged. Dorothy shook her head. "Goodness, I have no idea." She blew on her cold hands. "I see where you're going with this, Annie. Brilliant!"

Juice's brow wrinkled. "What's brilliant?"

Audie was uncertain herself.

"Don't you see?" Dorothy lowered her voice. "Here I am, free as a bird. And my uncle has not received a ransom note. For all practical purposes, no kidnapping has taken place."

"My thoughts, exactly," said Audie.

Juice scratched his head. "Have you lost your minds? Do you want those two to get off the hook?"

Of course, Audie wanted the Commodore and his cronies brought to justice. But what if they were denied the prestige of a kidnapping? What if they were brought up on different charges? She explained this proposition to Juice, Dorothy nodding all the while.

"All right, then." Juice straightened his shoulders. "I am not proud of this, but I am able to render invaluable assistance at this juncture in our adventure." He put his fingers to his lips. "But I must wait for the opportune time."

Audie exchanged a look with Dorothy. "What kind of assistance?" she asked.

"I would prefer not to say."

The look on her friend's face made it clear to Audie that the topic was not to be pursued. She nodded and the three huddled closer together against the cold, Juice sharpening his attention on the Commodore.

Step. Step. Step.

Now the line mounted the stairs, under the portico. Audie had never seen such a grand door, with roses carved over the arching entrance and Easter-egg-colored bits of jeweled glass inset in the panels. She caught her breath when she stepped inside. On every surface rested huge vases overflowing with roses and carnations and ferns. Audie closed her eyes to permanently imprint this memory. She couldn't wait to tell the Wayward Girls. Imagine— Audacity Jones in the White House proper! The triplets would no doubt cry tears of joy. Bimmy would shake her curly head. Divinity would, of course, cast aspersions as to the veracity of Audie's story.

But she really was here.

Step. Step. Step.

Each footfall brought her closer to the President.

And closer to the moment of truth.

CHAPTER THIRTY-FIVE

Nooses and Neckties

Charlie gave himself ten minutes in this getup. Fifteen minutes, tops. Then he would pass clean out.

"Mother, do I have to wear a tie?" He tugged at his collar, scarcely able to breathe.

Mrs. Taft beamed at her youngest. "You look so handsome, darling."

"Entirely dapper," added Helen. Charlie's sister admired herself in the mirror over the mantel in the Red Room, fussing with a poufy bit of hair above her ears. She'd changed her gown four times before deciding on the dusty pink one with the ridiculous white-feathered headband. "Cousin Dorothy will be positively taken."

Charlie groaned at his sister's remark.

"Where is she?" Helen asked. "Odd to be sleeping so late. Especially after missing supper last night."

Mrs. Taft exchanged a sharp glance with her husband. "She's not . . . not feeling well. I'm sure we'll see her soon." The capitol police force was quietly searching for the girl at this very moment.

It was probably only a little temper tantrum. That's what Detective Hill-Long had said. "Twelve-year-old girls are bundles of emotion," he'd told them. "No sense upsetting the apple cart yet. Give us until the end of the reception tomorrow. Then we'll notify her parents and the press if necessary." But, Detective Hill-Long had added, he did not think such notification would be necessary.

Charlie recognized the look between his parents. He'd seen it often enough. They used it whenever they wanted to keep something from him. He couldn't imagine what could be going on, but if Dorothy was under the weather, that was jim-dandy with him.

"Oh, dear." Mrs. Taft bent to take a closer look at her son's tie. "Is that a spot?"

Charlie wiped at the bit of dried egg yolk. "I told you I shouldn't dress before breakfast."

Mrs. Taft placed her hands on his shoulders. "Run upstairs, and put on a clean tie. Scoot."

Charlie sighed but did as he was told. He could never disobey his beloved mother. He took the stairs two at a time. Luckily, he'd left his bureau drawer open so it was easy to pull out a clean tie. Tying a Windsor knot was another story altogether. He stood in front of the mirror opposite the window and tried to remember the steps. He got the first loop and was wrestling with making the second loop—the wide end of the tie kept getting twisted—when he heard a noise. He stared in the mirror and there, over his shoulder at the window, a chocolate-striped cat batted against the pane.

He tugged on the knot as he approached the casement. "Do you want in, kitty?" Charlie carefully nudged the window open, so as not to knock the cat down. "Mother's not that fond of animals," he warned as the cat lifted its delicate long legs over the sill and pounced into the room. "You better wait here till I get back." Charlie reached down and scratched behind the cat's ears. "It's going to be a long time, I'm sorry to say. Big doings today." He got the spare blanket from the closet and made a nest on the floor. "You can sleep here," Charlie offered. "I'll bring you some food as soon as I can." He put a finger to his lips. "But keep it down or it's out you go."

The cat blinked its golden eyes at him, as if it understood every-thing he said.

Charlie dashed out the door, this time with a lighter step than minutes before. He could hardly keep the grin off his face as he entered the Red Room where his family was gathered.

"Well, don't you look like the cat that swallowed the canary," Helen teased.

"Slow down, son," President Taft said. "Let's show a little decorum."

Charlie slowed, and moved with as much decorum as a boy who had miraculously snagged a pet cat could. He could not resist one glance toward the stairs. He would make his way to his room as soon as was humanly possible.

Mrs. Taft gave her family one last inspection, nodding to indi-cate her satisfaction. "Shall we go?"

And at the moment the clock struck eleven, they lined up to greet the earliest of their hundreds of morning guests. The First Family was accompanied by Agent Sloan and his small detail of Secret Service men—though today there were four agents in all instead of the usual three. The agents stationed themselves in their pre-arranged places.

By the time the Tafts had greeted every member of the diplomatic corps, the thrill of the costumes and accents had dulled for Charlie. His legs ached from standing, but if Mother was still on her feet, he had to be, too. If only Quentin Roosevelt could have come. They would have found some way to entertain themselves. Maybe they would've talked the Ambassador from Chile into letting them hold his sword. Or maybe they would've tied together the shoelaces of that sleepy-eyed Secret Service agent behind the ferns. Or maybe he and Quentin would have snuck away so Charlie could show off his new cat.

Charlie's stomach rumbled as the last of the diplomats passed by and the first of the citizens began filing through. The sound was so loud that the Ambassador from China jumped a foot off the ground.

Mother frowned at him.

"I can't help it," Charlie whispered. "I'm hungry."

"Me too," said President Taft.

His wife glowered at him. "You can wait," she said. Then she turned to Charlie. "Run on down to the kitchen and ask Mrs. Jaffray for a sandwich to tide you over until the luncheon."

"Thank you, Mother!" Charlie waited for a break in the advancing column of citizens and ducked through the State Dining Room, planning to make a beeline for the first-floor pantry. Mrs. Jaffray had stationed herself there during the reception.

Charlie edged along the far wall of the dining room, and was about to step through the doorway into the pantry when he saw a familiar face. That girl, the one he'd run over with his bicycle. She was with a Negro footman about Charlie's age, and another girl. *That* girl looked familiar, too. He stared. Though she was decked out in some kind of kitchen maid's clothes, it was Dorothy! What on earth was going on? Wasn't she ill? Were these three playing some sort of prank? Charlie ducked behind a pillar.

This boring reception was looking up!

CHAPTER THIRTY-SIX

The President's Reception

As the disguised threesome scuffed closer and closer to the President, the First Lady, and most of the Tafts—Charlie was missing from the receiving line—Audie continued to refine their plan of action. Its goal was ambitious: to find a way to safely return Dorothy to her family *and* reveal the Commodore's dastardly plot at the same time, without giving him the dubious honor of having successfully kidnapped the President's niece. Though the Commodore was behind everything, Cypher, Mrs. Finch, and that bellman must also be dealt with.

Audie stuck her hand in her pocket, her fingers encountering the rosette there. The Commodore's fortunes had likely taken a nosedive with the popularity of the automobile. And President Taft's passion for the four-wheeled rather than the four-legged form of transportation would certainly make him unpopular with the Commodore. Audie could see that. She could fathom, too, how a downturn in fortune would also injure his pride. But there were many to whom bad fortune had fallen who had not resorted to dishonorable measures.

And what assurance had the Commodore that his plan for ransom would work? She reflected on Daddy Dub's story about President Grant. Simply because someone was President didn't mean they were rich.

Audie snuck another glance at the Commodore, several feet ahead of her, patting his own coat pocket.

Her ear tingled all the more. Even a bungling criminal like the Commodore would surely find a solution more sensible than delivering the note while in the receiving line. Though Audie discussed possibilities with Dorothy and Juice, she could not imagine what the Commodore's plan entailed.

Juice, however, had surmised a reasonable option. One that he preferred to keep from his two companions, lest they think ill of him. He had decided the time had come to put to use the skills learned from his light-fingered cousin during that brief but wretched period in his care. At least, this time, he would be doing a bad thing for a good reason.

Holding his finger up to Audie and Dorothy, signaling them to wait where they were, Juice straightened his clothing and edged his way up the line, where he accidentally on purpose bumped into the Commodore.

"Oh, pardon me, sir." Juice tipped his cap and backed away. "I was playing with a nickel and it rolled right by your feet."

"Watch what you're doing," Mrs. Finch snapped.

"He's only a boy," the Commodore said, patting her arm. "No harm done."

"Thank you, sir. Dreadfully sorry, sir." Juice tipped his hat again and quickly made his way back to Audie and Dorothy.

Juice gave Audie the biggest wink. She cocked her head, mystified, but completely trusting her friend. What happened next would depend on the Commodore. She fixed her eye on him as he greeted Mrs. Taft and stepped closer to the President.

Though we pride ourselves on having provided a reliable reporting of the events thus far, the details of the next few moments are difficult to accurately portray. One really needed to be present. The following are the facts as best as can be shared.

The Commodore, his white hair in stark contrast to his black coat and hat, stepped forward, his right hand outstretched to clasp the President's, while his left hand went to his vest pocket. That motion caused two men to appear out of nowhere. They pounced on the Commodore while the President swept his wife and daughter out of harm's way.

One of the tacklers was a man of amazing girth, who, despite having been several yards in line behind the Commodore, executed a fantastic series of leaps and tumbles to cover the space as if it did not exist. Another one of tacklers was a man with raven-black hair, who, not fifteen minutes before, had been deputized into the White House Secret Service.

"Drop it!" Cypher ordered. In a series of incidents much too complicated to explain here, the erstwhile chauffeur turned national hero. There may be some who were surprised by the chauffeur's bold actions, but not Detective Hill-Long, who deputized him, and certainly not the Shah of Persia, whose life had been saved not once but thrice by this very chauffeur prior to his leaving that country because of a broken heart. Had Cypher been overly unkind to a certain young orphan, or had he acted out of grave concern for her safety? That you must judge for yourself.

"Drop what?" The Commodore raised his hands above his head. "I've nothing. Nothing." He turned to search for Mrs. Finch, all the while muttering, "I don't understand. It's gone. Where did it go?"

During the kerfluffle, Mrs. Finch had been slowly and steadily backing away from her associate. She had nearly achieved the corridor, with a clear shot to the East Room's exit and freedom, when a blur of fur scrabbled across the parquet floor, and leapt atop her hat, ripping the stuffed bird clean off.

"Good on you, Min!" Audie called. She joined her four-footed friend in the chase of the phony cook, grabbing the hem of her skirt, which she tugged as hard as she could to stymie an escape.

"It was all her idea!" The Commodore pointed at the now hysterical Mrs. Finch, who was thumping Audie with her pocketbook. Audie did not think she could hold on much longer when a petite woman in a emerald velvet dress appeared and gazed into Mrs. Finch's eyes.

"*Állj!*" The tiny woman said in nearly perfect English, "Stop." And Mrs. Finch did. At that moment, two more Secret Service agents popped up, each grabbing one of Mrs. Finch's flailing arms.

"You'd both better come with us," one of the agents said.

The Commodore looked at Cypher. "Tell them. Tell them you work for me!"

Cypher folded his arms across his chest. "The truth is, Stinky, now I work for him." And with the first smile Audie had ever seen on his stern face, Cypher pointed at the President.

"And I thought this day was going to be a total snooze," Charlie exclaimed. "Hot dog!"

Dorothy flew into her aunt's arms.

Mrs. Taft held her tight, kissing the top of her head. "Where have you been, dear girl? What have you been through?"

Dorothy returned the hug and then broke away long enough to gesture to Audie and Juice. "I was kidnapped," she said. "And they saved me."

* * *

Tea was served up in the Blue Room, along with tears and laughter at the fantastic turn of events. Understandably fatigued, considering the situation and her health, Mrs. Taft had not moved from her seat by the grand fireplace as the story was unraveled for all. Audie started with the Commodore's arrival at Miss Maisie's School for Wayward Girls.

"She let you go off with that man?" Mrs. Taft exclaimed.

Audie felt compelled to come to Miss Maisie's defense. "I was game to go. And I don't think he ever intended to harm me. That was all Mrs. Finch's doing."

At that name, Mrs. Jaffray sniffed. "She made the worst Terrapin Soup ever."

"Between that and our worry over Dorothy, I went through an entire tin of bicarbonate." The President belched. Out of deference to his office, no one remarked on the sound.

"Well, there's no more need to worry." Cypher looked altogether dashing in his brand-new uniform. "It'll be a while before Stinky Crutchfield gets out of prison." He exchanged glances with

Beatrice, who had been sent for at the hotel. Her cheeks bloomed the most charming shade of pink.

"I don't understand how you worked it all out," Mrs. Taft said to Audie.

"I couldn't have done it without Bimmy and the Punish—the library," Audie replied. "You can find every bit of information you'd ever need there. Including vital particulars about circuses." At this juncture, she nodded at Madame Volta and Igor. "I can't thank you enough."

"*Szóra sem érdemes,*" Madame Volta inclined her petite head. "It was nothing. Our pleasure."

Igor smiled. "Ve came zee moment ve got zee telegram from Bimmy. Circus friends are bound by sawdust and iron," he said, flexing his arm slightly.

Madame Volta stood, smoothing out her emerald velvet skirt. "And now, we must take our leave. We have a performance at six this evening. You are all welcome!"

"Hot dog!" cried Charlie.

"Not today, I'm afraid," said his mother. But she made plans to send him the very next week and he had a glorious time as the special guest of Madame Volta.

"Farewell. *Isten veled.*" Madame Volta clasped Audie's hands. "Give my love to Bimmy when next you see her." With that, she and Igor were gone.

"You are simply amazing, my dear." Mrs. Taft turned her warm and lovely smile on Audie.

"Well, I couldn't have accomplished anything without my friends." Thoughts of Bimmy and the triplets, who had conquered their fears to enter the Punishment Room, filled her heart. Then she caught Juice's gaze. "Friends old and new," she said.

"How clever and brave of you to pick the Commodore's pocket," Dorothy said to Juice.

He shrugged. "I'm not proud that I have a talent for light-fingeredness, but I'm glad I could put it to good use."

"How do you think we should reward this pair?" the President asked his wife.

"Oh, please, let's find Audie a real home!" Dorothy said. She had finally been alerted as to Audacity's real name. "Maybe here in town. That way I could see her often!" She clasped Audie's arm and hugged it close.

Charlie did not even groan at that suggestion. In fact, he thought life in the White House would be ever so much more lively if Audie accompanied Dorothy on her next visit.

"Oh, thank you so much." Audie pressed her hand to her heart. "But I must be getting back. I have responsibilities at Miss Maisie's."

The President waved Cypher over and the two of them spoke in low tones. "It's settled," said President Taft. "Cypher will drive Audie—"

"And Beatrice!" Audie inserted.

"And Beatrice back to Swayzee. In my brand-new touring car. Just the vehicle for a long journey."

Beatrice clapped her hands. "*Merci*, monsieur! *Merci*."

Audie could see a cloud behind Juice's smile of happiness for her. "I wonder . . ." She chewed on her bottom lip. "What's going to happen to the Commodore's car?"

The President shrugged. "It'll be sold at auction, I imagine. He won't have any use for it where he's going."

Audie wiggled the toes in her left boot. There was something she'd discuss with the President later. For now, she was exhausted. She wanted a hot bath, a croissant, and a good night's sleep before beginning the drive home. She hugged Dorothy. "We'll write," she said. "And you'll visit if you ever come to Swayzee."

Dorothy gave her a squeeze and reluctantly let her go. "I'll never forget you."

* * *

Though he lived to be an old man with droopy earlobes and teeth that clicked when he talked, after that New Year's Day White House reception, Charlie Taft never ever again thought that girls were boring. Not for an instant.

CHAPTER THIRTY-SEVEN

And Macarons, to Boot

The front wheel jolted into a pothole, startling Audie awake from her dream. And such a pleasant one, too. There had been a man and a woman, their faces dappled by the shadows of the apple trees in the orchard through which the three of them strolled. Audie's right arm was wrapped around the woman's waist. And the woman's right arm was tucked into the man's left. The three were twined together like roses, jasmine, and ivy woven in a bridal wreath. The woman spoke a word: *daughter.* It lingered in the cool air like a perfect clear note, growing ever fainter with each blink of Audie's fluttering eyelids.

"We're almost there," Cypher called over his shoulder. As *her* mission was no longer secret, Min proudly rode in the front passenger seat, golden eyes keenly focused on the road. The whole dangerous affair of the Commodore and the kidnapping was well behind them but the cat was determined to remain alert nevertheless.

Audie blinked one last time. Those pleasing parental dream shapes dissolved like sugar granules in a cup of hot tea. The sweetness of her dream would linger briefly, and then disappear. That thought forced a bit of hot moisture to prick at the backs of Audie's eyes. She shook it away. Bees and bonnets! What had she to be sad about today?

She smiled to think of her farewell to Daddy Dub. He told her that Samuel had given Selma a new lease on life, the two of them playing like foals.

Parting company with Juice had proved bittersweet, with him so down in the dumps at Audie's departure. Wait until he saw that robin's egg blue automobile parked in front of the stables, thanks to President Taft. That fine car would get him all the way to Seattle, or wherever he dreamed of going. And she hoped that when he headed west, he would make a stop at a certain School for Wayward Girls.

Audie wiggled her toes in her boots, with one gold coin gone to a good cause. She inclined her head to the right, away from the window, away from the view of rural Indiana, and the signs that they were approaching Swayzee—the rolling fields, the copses of hickory trees dotting those fields, the bright, flat sky—to look at her current travel companion. One whose presence perfumed the air with yeast and buttery warmth and the occasional *macaron* when the situation warranted.

Beatrice returned Audie's smile. She folded and unfolded her hands in her lap. "What if Miss Maisie does not have the usefulness for me?"

Cypher chuckled from his place behind the steering wheel. Audie patted the box on the seat next to her. "Once she gets one taste of your *petits fours*, she is going to be your best friend. For life."

"They are almost as delicious as my mother's baklava," added Cypher.

Beatrice's cheeks turned that charming shade of Parisian pink and she ducked her head, shy as a schoolgirl going to her first tea dance. "You are too kind," she said. But she began to hum that lovely song that had soothed Audie to sleep the many nights since their first meeting.

Audie leaned back, going over again in her mind the plan she'd concocted in those last desperate minutes when she had realized she could not leave poor Beatrice behind in Washington, D.C. Beatrice needed song sparrows to awaken her each morning, wooded lanes to stroll each afternoon, and mourning doves to coo her to sleep each night. It will not come as a surprise to you, dear reader, that our heroine quickly arrived at an exquisite solution: Beatrice would teach the Wayward Girls a trade. They would learn to bake. Of course, not all of them could be as skilled as she. Actually, few of them could be. But Audie secretly thought the triplets might have the cool hands required for proper croissants and that, underneath her cross and prickly exterior, Divinity might be enough of a romantic to do justice to éclairs.

They would start small at first. Perhaps with a table at the Methodist Mission Bazaar. Later, they'd sell goods at Mr. Sharp's General Store. Perhaps one day, the baked goods of the Wayward Girls would grace the tables at the White House. As Audie knew all too well, stranger things had happened.

She smiled again at Beatrice, then turned her gaze outward, catching a glimpse of that stooped old white pine. They would soon be upon Miss Maisie's. Audie peered out, straining for a first glimpse of Bimmy, of Violet, of Lavender, of Lilac. Of Cook. Of Miss Maisie. Even of Divinity.

Min was hard-pressed to contain her excitement as well. She leapt over the seat into Audie's skirt, rubbing her head on the underside of Audie's chin, kneading her lap.

"There it is, Min!" Audie leaned forward, catching sight of the big bay window on the main floor that had been her port in so many storms. Not Punishment Room but refuge. Or as was written above the great library at Alexandria, *A Place of Healing for the Soul.* And now she wasn't the only Wayward Girl who knew that truth.

A movement caught Audie's eye, causing her to shift her gaze, and into view came a slight figure, running along the lane, toward the automobile. The sight of that figure—dark curls bouncing, welcome and joy in that broad smile—caused her heart to overflow and leak from her eyes. "Bimmy!" Audie thrust her arms out the window, calling to her bosom friend. "Bimmy! Oh, Bimmy. We're home." Audie drew her arms in and snatched Min to her chest, holding her close.

"I'm home."

✳CHAPTER THIRTY-EIGHT✳

P.S.

Audie was reading aloud from Little Women while Beatrice supervised a lesson on kneading baguette dough.

"Audie! Audie!" Bimmy waved something in her hand. "You got a postcard from Cypher."

Audie calmly marked her place in the book and took the postcard from her friend. On one side was a photograph of that famous magician, Harry Houdini.

"May I see?" Violet reached for it with floury hands.

"After you wash up," Audie said gently. Her ear began to buzz as she reversed the card to read aloud the note on the back. In Cypher's bold block print were these words: WISH YOU WERE HERE.

"Oh, dear." Audie looked over Violet's head to Beatrice. They exchanged a meaningful glance. "I guess I'd best pack a bag."

Author's Note

Some years ago, I was minding my own business, working on another project, when the image of an eleven-year-old girl, in a long dress and kid-leather boots, popped into my mind. She lay on her stomach on a carpet in front of a fire, reading a book. Her name was Audacity and she lived up to it by demanding that I immediately set aside what I was working on in order to transfer the scene in my mind to the page. I wrote several hundred words and then put them away. I fell in love with Audie from the start, but had no idea what her story was.

That is until, on a lark, I wondered about the headlines on January 1, 1910 (these things happen when you are passionate about the past). I got online and pulled up several old newspapers and there I found the story of the "kidnapping" of Dorothy Taft, the daughter of then-President Taft's cousin (that is one of the changes I made to this story: Dorothy was a shirttail relation, rather than a niece). The girl went missing in Los Angeles (not Washington, D.C.) on the way home from a visit to a friend. I thought I'd found pure historic gold until I read the papers of January 2, 1910, and learned that Dorothy had been quickly reunited with her family; the "disappearance" a result of a misunderstanding about train times.

Well, there goes my story, I thought. But, again, Audie had other ideas. She nudged her way to the front of my mind and asked my favorite writer's question: What if? What if Dorothy had been kidnapped? Who might have done such a deed? And why? And couldn't a resourceful and well-read girl like Audie somehow be involved in her rescue? These questions seemed not only reasonable but requiring of answers. The book you are holding in your hand is my attempt to answer them.

This is a work of historical fiction. In the service of this story, I have taken many more creative liberties than I usually do. Here are the facts: President Taft did have blue eyes and was mad for automobiles; his wife, Nellie, had visited the White House as a teen and longed to live there; her dream did come true but at a cost to her health. She suffered a stroke shortly after her husband's inauguration and it was months before she recovered enough to play White House hostess. Her memoir, *Recollections of Full Years* (1914), took me inside the Taft White House. Mrs. Jaffray was one of Mrs. Taft's first hires and her book, *Secrets of the White House* (1926), was invaluable to me; that's where I learned that Mrs. Taft loved to wear violets, and that a special English cook was always hired to prepare Terrapin Soup for the President. Though I have no knowledge that he was ever called Daddy Dub, Mr. W. W. Brown was indeed a White House livery driver, starting in the administration of President Grant, working through President Taft's—fifty-six years! The story he tells about President Grant is true, though of course, I do not know if Mr. Brown ever related it to anyone. He certainly never related it to Juice, because that wonderful newsboy is a completely invented character.

The books that Audie takes with her on her journey are invented as well; dear friends will recognize themselves as authors (other dear friends will discover themselves elsewhere in this book). The excerpt Audie reads in Chapter Ten is not from the [imaginary] book *Fair Criminals, Foul Minds*, but from *The Right Way to Do Wrong: An Exposé of Successful Criminals*, written by Harry Houdini and published in 1906.

There is a town called Swayzee, Indiana (thank you, Katy Van Aken, for all the help with learning about your town in 1910, and to Brooklyn and Kiley for being such supportive and enthusiastic fans), but Miss Maisie's School for Wayward Girls and its inhabitants are works of fiction, though Audie and her friends seem very real to me.

Acknowledgments

A huge debt of gratitude goes to the Washington Historical Society; the White House Historical Association, especially Mr. William Bushong; Katy Van Aken for inspiration, encouragement, and all things Swayzee; and Tricia Gort Kiepert and Nóra Hajdu for assistance with the Hungarian phrases.

I'm often asked where my characters come from. Sometimes I know. Sometimes I don't. Audie is rooted in a little girl who wore hand-me-downs and was the new kid in school more times than she could count; a child who learned the hard way that sometimes friends were only to be found within the covers of a book.

This story is for all of the adults who nurtured that little girl: my loving parents, who not only didn't mind that their eldest was a bit odd, they loved her all the more for it; the librarians who gave me books and got out of the way; the teachers—especially you, Mr. Craig!—who took note; the Camp Fire moms who mentored me: Barbara Duncan, Mary Lou Maybee, Rhoda Patterson, and Lucille Young. Make new friends, but keep the old.

I say this every time but only because it's true: I couldn't write a word without Mary Nethery or without the support of my patient husband, Neil. Thanks to my children: Tyler, Nicole, Eli, and Audrey; Quinn, Matt, and Esme; I love you all. And nothing I write would ever see the light of day without my lionhearted agent, Jill Grinberg, and her Brooklyn crew, Cheryl Pientka, Katelyn Detwiler, and Denise St. Pierre.

My gratitude to the Scholastic family for supporting my passion for historical fiction is unending (here's hoping they never wise up): Thank you, publicity and marketing wizards including Jennifer Abbots, Julie Amitie, Bess Brasswell, Michelle Campbell, Caitlin Friedman, Antonio Gonzalez, Emily Heddleson, Whitney Steller, Tracy Van Straaten, the fabulous sales team, and my buddy, Lizette Serrano; to Lori Benton, Ellie Berger, David Levithan, and Dick Robinson; Rebekah Wallin, production editor; Alan Boyko, Robin Hoffman, and the whole Book Fair crew. Belated thanks to Jenni Holm, who turned down a chance to write for the Dear America series, recommending me instead. That generous act led to my getting paired up with Lisa Sandell, a really sharp editor and now treasured friend. And last but not least, I thank you, dear reader, for giving me these precious hours of your life. *Köszönöm.*

About the Author

KIRBY LARSON is the acclaimed author of the 2007 Newbery Honor book *Hattie Big Sky*; its sequel, *Hattie Ever After*; *The Friendship Doll*; Dear America: *The Fences Between Us*; *Duke*; and *Dash*, winner of the Scott O'Dell Award for Historical Fiction. She has also cowritten two award-winning picture books: *Two Bobbies: A True Story of Hurricane Katrina, Friendship, and Survival*, and *Nubs: The True Story of a Mutt, a Marine & a Miracle*. Kirby lives in Washington State with her husband and Winston the Wonder Dog.